Carolyn

You've been a wonderful friend to our family. Thank you for all your support & the love you've shown in the difficult last few months with Mom.

I hope you enjoy "Bird"

Love,
Kim

Bird

A NOVEL

Kim E. Wilson

DEDICATION

In loving memory of my parents Stan and Joyce,
and to my greatest love, my husband Marty.

One PRESENT DAY

By the time I reached my destination, I was stiff and exhausted. Having spent the last ten hours on the road with my traveling companion Lilly, a lovable three-year-old retriever, I was ready for this journey to end. I still wasn't sure what I was doing here. The events of the last few weeks seemed like a dream, and yet, here I was, baffled at my own decision to come, and come alone, to a place I had never been before. People are scammed all the time. So, when I received a phone call from some guy claiming to be a Georgia attorney, contacting me on behalf of his deceased client regarding an inheritance that was left to me, I laughed. I told him he either had the wrong person, or his scam wasn't going to work. I hung up. Then came a registered letter from James P. Carmichael from Cameron, Carmichael and

Associates, in Brunswick, Georgia. Same attorney, same firm. I didn't believe it. Even after contacting my attorney and forwarding him the letter, I didn't believe it.

"Hey, girl, what do you think I'm getting myself into?" I said while glancing into the rearview mirror at my panting ball of fur in the back seat. Why would someone I had never known leave me anything, let alone a ten-acre estate in Brunswick, Georgia? *What on earth...? It's gotta be some mistake.* No, I knew it simply was a mistake. They've got the wrong Ellen Williams. I googled the law firm to see if it was legit. It seemed to be. I even called the number listed on the website, and, sure enough, someone answered.

"Cameron, Carmichael and Associates, how may I help you?" answered a pleasant female voice.

"I, ugh, I'm so sorry," I stammered. "I must have dialed the wrong number." I hung up.

I'm not sure why I didn't just ask for the lawyer who had sent me the letter. Why didn't I try and verify if he was a lawyer with that firm? Maybe I felt it was best left to someone who was better equipped to inquire into the legality of it all, like our family attorney, Greg Blackburn. If someone was scamming folks, chances are that Greg could find out for me. I called Greg and explained to him what was outlined in the letter and asked him to get back to me at his convenience. I told him I was sure it was a scam of some kind. He asked me to forward him a PDF of the letter, and he'd check into it. And a few days later, he called me back.

"Hi, Ellen, Greg Blackburn here. I've got some news for you, and I hope you're sitting down. It's legitimate. I've spoken to James Carmichael, the attorney for the estate of a Mrs. Madeline M. Caldwell. He confirms that you are the sole beneficiary of her Brunswick property, and I've obtained a copy of her will. Mr. Carmichael stated that she was very much of sound mind when the will was revised a couple of years ago. She and her husband had been a prominent couple in Brunswick. Judge Anderson Caldwell had served over forty years on the bench. Mrs. Caldwell did volunteer work and fundraising for local charities and was president and co-founder of the Brunswick Women's Club. She updated her will long after the judge died in 2008. So, it looks like you're the proud owner of a ten-acre property in Brunswick, Georgia."

Greg has been our attorney since Dan and I became parents. That was thirty-five years ago. Since, we've had two children and lost three of our parents—everyone except my still fairly healthy eighty-five-year-old mother. I trusted him explicitly, but I was still having a hard time believing what he was telling me.

"And Ellen, the property itself is estimated at 7.8 million dollars. She also provided an additional two million dollars to offset the taxes. It looks like the angels have smiled upon you. Can I maybe get on your Christmas list this year?" He asked with a laugh.

I was too stunned to respond to his attempt at humor. I do remember asking him to repeat everything at least two more times.

"Greg, I hear you, but I don't believe any of this. It just doesn't make sense. This kind of thing doesn't happen! This is just fucking ridiculous, I mean, sorry, well, you know what I mean."

He chuckled. "I know, it's pretty extraordinary."

"What about family, surely they had family to leave this to?"

"According to her lawyer, the Caldwells had no children, only a nephew on the judge's side of the family. His sister's boy. Wait a minute, I've written his name down, let me see. Oh, here it is, a Doctor Hunter McGaffey. Yes, he was the only child born to the judge's younger sister, and he unfortunately lost both of his parents in a tragic car accident a few years back. Hold on, let me just confirm that." After a few seconds he came back on the line. "Yes, I've got that correct. The nephew's a cardiac surgeon in Brunswick who's divorced and has two daughters, ages nineteen and seventeen. Mr. Carmichael said that Mrs. Caldwell left her nephew around ten million dollars in cash and stocks and the great nieces received two million dollars apiece to be received on their twenty-first birthdays. The girls were also given the option of using all or part of the money for their education before turning twenty-one. Dr. McGaffey is the executor of their trust and will oversee the distribution of his daughters' portions. Mrs. Caldwell also gave a sizeable donation to her favorite charities and set up an endowment at Emory University under the judge's name. Mr. Carmichael did say that he is 99.9 percent sure that you are the correct recipient of the house and grounds."

"I'm totally at a loss, Greg. There must be some reason she didn't leave it all to her family or other charities, or the endowment. Why in heaven's name would she leave it to a total stranger?" I asked, totally mystified. "It just doesn't make sense."

His next words truly chilled me.

"Well, whether you are a stranger to her or not, you are the intended recipient. And the reason I know: she left proof. A photograph of you," he stated.

My heart began to pound, and my palms began to sweat. I'm not sure I heard him correctly. "Photograph, what photograph?"

He proceeded to tell me that her lawyer had forwarded him not only a copy of the will, but a picture of me. He said it was Mrs. Caldwell's way of letting me know that I was the intended beneficiary. She evidently told her lawyer that when the time came, she knew that I would need proof.

"Give me a minute, and I'll forward you the email with the attachments. I didn't want to send it without talking to you first. I thought you might faint. Okay, give me a sec. Alright, it's on its way. Check your inbox. I've got to run, Ellen. But let me know what I can do to further help. You'll most likely have questions down the road. I would also suggest that you get a hold of a good accountant at some point. I have a few names I can recommend if you'd like," he said.

"Oh, right, well I've got my CPA for the business, so I can reach out to him. Listen, thanks so much. I'm sure I'll be in touch." I said.

"Anytime. Take care."

"You too, Greg."

I put down the phone and moved to my laptop. My hands shook as I opened Greg's email. There were two attachments, one entitled "Last Will and Testament of Madeline M. Caldwell" and the other entitled "Photo." I decided I'd look at the will after I looked at the photo. I clicked on "Photo." It took a few seconds to open, but when it did, my brain exploded as I tried to process the image before me. There was no doubt it was me. I think I must have stood there for a solid minute staring at the screen. It took me another minute to race through the halls of my memory and recall where the picture had been taken. I was standing in front of a large fountain in a park- like setting. My hair was styled similar to the way I wear it now, a short, messy blond crown of natural waves. I was smiling for the camera. The thing I noticed first was that this slightly younger version of myself was smiling, yet still looked rather sad. My arms reflected a summer tan, and I was wearing a bright lime green sleeveless blouse and a pair of white capris. I bought that blouse in a little boutique in Midway, Kentucky, with Sharon, my best friend of over twenty years. We were on one of our girl trips. But Midway was not where the picture was taken. I racked my brain trying to remember where we were. I've always hated trying to navigate those cerebral corridors. And then, it hit me. I suddenly remembered where this picture was taken. We were in Forsyth Park in Savannah, Georgia. It was just one of the many vacations Sharon and I had taken together. This trip was kind of a mini four-day getaway. We had been looking forward to discovering the city with cocktails, sunshine, and laughter on the menu. Then came the phone call from someone I hadn't seen or spoken to in years. My sister.

Two 2016

"Ellen, your phone's ringing! Ellen!!" Sharon yelled over the hum of the hair dryer. "It's Jenny."

"Who?"

"Jenny."

I stood there, frozen, one hand holding the hotel blow-dryer, and the other clutching a round brush. Jenny. Jenny was calling. I hadn't heard from her in, my God, how many years now? Why the hell was she calling me? I turned the dryer off and walked over to the phone. My hands trembled as I held it, feeling the vibration as I let it ring.

"Aren't you going to answer it?" Sharon asked as she applied sunscreen to her face.

I stood there, clutching the phone. It had been too long. I wouldn't know what to say to my sister after all these years. I guess I must have waited long enough because it stopped ringing. I was holding my breath, and, when it stopped, I slowly exhaled. A feeling of both relief and sadness washed over me.

"What do you think she wants?"

"I have no idea." I said.

"Did she leave a voicemail?"

I laughed, but not from joy. "Jenny doesn't leave voicemails. Ghosts don't leave voicemails."

"Aren't you even a little bit curious about what she might want?"

"No. Maybe. Shit. I don't know," I said as I put the phone back on the hotel desk and sat down.

My older sister was a mystery to our entire family. Jenny was a live ghost, haunting us with her minimal presence throughout the years, only to vanish for long periods of time, years even. Drifting in and out of our lives, usually inflicting collateral damage on one or more of us. Each time she walked in, I hoped there might be some semblance of a relationship, but she would disappear again, just vanish without so much as an explanation. I didn't trust her anymore with my heart. How many times had she walked away from me when I needed her? I would capitulate and give her another chance, only to be betrayed. The last time I spoke with her I told her I was done. That there was nothing left for us to build a relationship on. I wished her well and said goodbye.

I grabbed a tissue off the desk and held it to my face, on the verge of tears that never came. I hadn't shed tears for Jenny in a long time.

"It's probably just another one of her tricks. I'm not wasting anymore of my time. Let her haunt someone else," I said, getting up to return to drying my still-damp hair and keep it from frizzing any further. I hadn't taken more than a few steps when the phone began to buzz again. I stopped and slowly turned around. Jenny's name appeared as the incoming call.

"Shit! It's her!"

This time, with just a moment of hesitation, I answered. "Hello?" I waited for a response. I knew she was there. I could somehow feel her on the other end. "Hello? Jenny. Jenny, I know it's you. What do you want? Are you alright?" I waited. A few seconds passed, and then a few more. I was about to hang up.

"*Ellen*," came the faintest of whispers across the line. I wasn't sure if I had truly heard my name, or just a voice inside my head.

I waited and then said, "Jenny, are you there?"

Nothing, no response. I looked at the phone. The call ended. I was angry and a bit scared. I didn't know if she was playing games with me or if she might really be in trouble. I tried returning the call several times but that proved futile.

"Should I call Jenny's husband? Should I call my

mother?" I asked Sharon. "I haven't talked to Mike in ages. I don't even have his number."

"What about your Mom? Do you think maybe she's heard from her?"

"Oh, God, I hate calling my mother about this. She's so bitter about Jenny. I don't think Mom's spoken to Jenny in ages. I'd be surprised if Mom knows anything, but…." I let the sentence trail off without finishing it.

"It might be worth a phone call to your mom," Sharon said.

"You're right, I should call her."

Mom picked up on the fifth ring, and my conversation with her went exactly as I expected. My eighty-five-year-old mother hadn't heard from Jenny. In fact, she hadn't heard from Jenny in over two years. It was always a difficult subject to broach with my mother because I knew how much it hurt her. She didn't know why her eldest daughter was estranged from the family, from her own mother. The last time any of us actually saw Jenny was my father's funeral. We were all surprised to see her. And, literally, that's all we did was see her. She spoke to no one. She must have drifted in after the service began. When it concluded, I willed myself to get up and move forward, not wanting this to be the final act for my father. Though my eyes were clouded with grief, I immediately recognized her. There she was, standing in the back of the room, staring straight in my direction. Jenny looked like an apparition. She was thinner than I'd ever seen her, gaunt even. Her unwashed shoulder-length hair had grayed dramatically. Hanging on her bony frame was a blue-jean button-down blouse and a shapeless khaki skirt. She just looked weathered and exhausted, like a tired old workhorse right before it's put out to pasture. I thought she might collapse. But then, she straightened up, threw her shoulders back, lifted her chin, and left. I didn't know what to make of it, other than thinking that Jenny felt the need to make an uncomfortable appearance. It was hard to care after all these years. It was apparent that the bitterness she carried reflected the physical woman I saw that day.

"Mom, do you have Mike's number, or maybe the number to their house phone? I don't have either. I'm out of town. Sharon and I are in Savannah, remember? So, there isn't much I can do from here. Do you think maybe you can do that, Mom? Try and reach Jenny or Mike? Just to make sure everything's okay?

"I suppose," she said with no emotion. "I think I've got their numbers in my address book. I'll have to look. Hold on."

I could hear her shuffling through pages of what was most likely her address book. After a few minutes, she came back on the line. "I found their house phone number. I can try that."

"Okay, that's good. I'll have my phone on me, so just let me know if you find anything out either way, okay?"

There was a long pause.

"Mom, okay?"

"Yes, I'll call."

I know she was feeling sad. Sadness for all the wasted years my sister chose to isolate herself. Sadness that her eldest daughter didn't so much as say a comforting word to her when she was burying a husband of sixty years. It was her own father, for Christ's sake. Who does that?

"Well, let me know if you find out anything either."

"All right," she said and hung up.

"Well, that's that. She hasn't heard from her, but she said she would try and call her," I said to Sharon.

I thought about my mom. It had to be hard on her to have a child that disconnected. As much as she tried, Mom couldn't understand why Jenny stayed away. I thought about Alex and Mia. Yes, I'd had my share of problems with my own children through the years, but I can't conceive of a world without them. But I know Mom was hurt, and I think in some way, Jenny enjoyed having that kind of power, the power to hurt.

It was now late morning in Savannah. I didn't want to waste any more time on something I could do nothing about.

"Well, how about we go do a bit of sightseeing and then find a place where we can enjoy a liquid lunch? I could use it," I said.

"Sounds like a great plan," Sharon laughed.

It was a gorgeous but already sweltering morning in Savannah. We had gotten in late the night before and had little time to do anything except grab a drink at the hotel bar and crash in the room. We were eager to see the city and decided we'd walk around in the morning and then find a nice place for lunch. The restaurant we chose wasn't far from the hotel, and we could cut straight across Forsyth Park. We took our time, strolling under the Georgia sun and enjoying the tranquility of the park. The massive oak trees were draped in blankets of luxurious Spanish moss which provided shade from what most assuredly was going to be stifling by the afternoon. I could understand how Savannah earned its name, The Forest City. The lush vegetation of the park made you feel a part of the landscape. Aside from the live oak trees, the park housed sweet gums, magnolias, as well as vibrant crepe myrtles. We could see a wedding party being photographed next to a magnolia. At the other end of the park was a group of young girls. They looked to be around five or six, each dressed in a variety of pastel party dresses trimmed in white lace. Possibly a birthday party with a tea party theme. The girls laughed and shouted at one another as they held hands and danced around a table covered in white linen and decorated with pink streamers. We eventually made our way to the fountain. The water looked cool and refreshing as it rose and fell, cascading like liquid glass that formed bubbles below. I don't know what Sharon was thinking, but I was wishing I could jump in.

"Turn around, I'll get your picture," Sharon said,

backing away so she could photograph me with the fountain behind me.

"Here, let me," said a middle-aged gentleman in a Panama hat who had been standing near the fountain. "I'll get this one, and then I'll get you both."

"Oh, perfect, thanks," Sharon said as she handed him her phone. He snapped a few pictures for us, both alone and together.

"Here ya go," he said, handing the phone back. "Hope they work for you."

We both thanked him and spent the next half hour wandering the grounds before lunch. It was almost noon and the back of my neck was more than damp. I was ready to find some air conditioning. We made our way to the restaurant that was just across from Forsyth Park, housed in a charming southern mansion named The Savannah Sisters. *Well, of course,* I thought, *I can't seem to escape "sisters" today.* We were escorted into a lovely dining area, where tall windows lined the room and a beautiful set of French doors led out to a white-columned terrace. The floors were a gleaming dark mahogany and contrasted remarkably with the faint robin's-egg blue that was chosen for the wall color. The room was light and airy, filled with giant ferns, sparkling crystal chandeliers, and a fabulous view of the park. From our table, we watched couples strolling and joggers, some with pets, some without, winding along the paths. It seemed surreal to me to be sitting in such a lovely place, when just moments ago I was in a dark hotel room trying to make a connection with the spirit of my estranged sister. She just wasn't real to me anymore.

The waitress had taken our drink orders, two glasses of Sauvignon Blanc to start and ice water. The wine couldn't come fast enough. We picked up our menus and began browsing the lunch entrées. In the left insert of the menu, there was a short introduction to the restaurant.

It began:

There once were two Savannah Sisters who inherited this very house from their wealthy father, a prominent businessman in Savannah in the late 1860s. The girls' mother died after giving birth to the second daughter. During the girls' teenage years, they shared the role of hostess whenever their father entertained. The girls were taught from an early age how to cook from the only caregiver they had ever known, Celia, a slave woman who had been with the family since before the girls were born. In the summer of 1866, their father died of influenza and his daughters were left to fend for themselves. To make matters worse, the girls learned that their father had lost most of his money in a land deal that went terribly wrong shortly before he died. Though he owned the house, he owed a large debt in back taxes. So, unless the girls could come up with the money to pay the taxes, they would have to sell the house. The girls negotiated a deal with the bank. If they turned the house into a small hotel and dining facility, they could pay the taxes within a year, along with an agreed upon interest rate. Reluctantly, the bank agreed. The girls opened The Savannah Sisters, paid the taxes before the year was out, and made their mark on Savannah society as one of the best establishments in town. Our menu reflects generations of southern family recipes, and our dishes are still prepared with the same traditions and care that we've used since the day the sisters opened for business. The Savannah Sisters hope you enjoy your meal.

Sisters. I remembered a time when my sister and I had been close. Jenny and I were once inseparable. We depended on each other. We promised we'd always be there for one another. I tried to keep my promise. She never did.

When our drinks arrived, we told the waitress we'd like to wait a bit before ordering lunch. We raised our glasses.

"Cheers!" we said simultaneously.

And then Sharon simply said, "Tell me about your sister."

Three

"Your destination is on your left in two hundred feet," the GPS flatly stated.

"Oh, shit, I gotta slow down." Braking and reducing my speed, I rolled down the window and let the humid Georgia air hit my face.

"Your destination is on your left." And so, here was the entrance to the Caldwell property. Twenty-foot hedges lined the left side of the road like sentries. I pulled into the entrance that was guarded by a massive set of black wrought-iron gates and positioned between two large stone columns. Each column simply bore the name Caldwell. I pulled up to the code box and punched in the numbers that were passed on to me by my lawyer. My hand was shaking so badly as I fumbled with the code that I was surprised when I heard the hum of a motor, then the click of the lock that slowly released the gate. I traveled down the tree-lined drive at a snail's pace. It was still early evening and the sun hadn't set. With the window rolled down I could smell summer and hear the cicadas' irritation at me for invading their quiet sanctuary. I took off my sunglasses so I could take in the colors, the richness of it all. I made my way deeper into the property. Glorious trees heavy with Spanish moss and flowering magnolias lined the drive. I know zero about botany, but I thought even the great Frank Olmsted, who had been responsible for the historical grounds of the Biltmore and even our local park in Louisville, would have been quite impressed. There was a large pond to the right. Numerous cattails etched the water's edge, and several ducks were bathing in this place of serenity. Now I was certain this was a mistake. Nobody, and I mean nobody, leaves this kind of property to a stranger. The driveway began to curve to the west and the setting sun bathed everything in muted gold. No sooner had I felt the warmth of the last of the evening rays on my face, when in front of me appeared the most charming house I think I had ever laid eyes on.

"Holy shit! I don't think we're in Kansas anymore, Toto!" I said to Lilly. "Wow, wow! Oh, my God! This just can't be real."

I pulled in to the circular driveway and put the car in park. For several seconds, I couldn't move. Just sat there. I finally came out of my stupor and reached for the door handle, practically falling out of the car. I stood there, using the car door to keep me upright as I took in what could only be a mirage. A house, so lovely, so utterly charming, I almost wept. Though it was most likely a mansion by anyone's standards, this stone beauty was the very definition of inviting. It was truly a vision. I was in a trance until Lilly gave me her loudest bark, notifying me that she was done with this car ride. Without taking my eyes off the house, I inched backward to free Lilly from incarceration. I opened the hatch and Lilly darted out, barely giving me enough time to grab her leash.

"Okay, girl. Hold on, hold on!"

Without waiting for permission, Lilly guided me from one bush to the next, thoroughly sniffing each leaf. I could only stare at the house and its surrounding property in disbelief. It didn't take Lilly long to take care of business, though I felt a little guilty that she showed such little respect for this beautiful lawn. But what's a dog to do? She decided it was time to sniff out the rest of the place. This seventy-five-pound beast began pulling me toward the house. I finally came to a complete stop, standing on the edge of the driveway, drinking in the scene. This house and its grounds were one of the most beautiful places I'd ever laid eyes on. A light stone the color of caramel was gleaming in the evening sun. The wide front steps led to a massive porch and appeared to wrap around the north side of the house. Large natural-colored wicker chairs had been placed in front of the large window and invited you to sit, relax, put your feet up, and have a glass of sweet tea. To the right was a porch swing that looked as if it had spent many a day rocking. I turned back and looked out to the front lawn. I couldn't explain it, but once again I got a lump in my throat and my eyes began to tear up. This was a house meant for family, for dogs and kids, mothers and fathers. It was built for love. It was a house for making memories. It was not a house you give away to a total stranger.

"What are we doing here, girl? What am I doing here? This is someone's home," I whispered walking back and plopping down on the front porch steps.

Lilly sat down next to me and put her head on my lap. I scratched behind her ears and looked out at this place, shaking my head, truly overwhelmed. Tears began to sting my eyes. Lately things seemed just too much. My marriage, the business, the family. I know the only reason I decided to do this alone was because I needed time to think, to make some hard decisions. The evening breeze began to blow with the scent of jasmine filling the air. An image appeared in my head of me sitting on another set of porch steps. It was my great-grandmother's farm. My favorite grandparent, Annabelle Lyons, but everyone called her Belle. She and my great-grandfather Clifford lived on a large forty-acre farm in Illinois. As a child, I would spend hours playing outside that farmhouse, climbing fences, and hiding in cornfields. How I loved that place. And when she died, they sold the farm. I was heartbroken. There was never anyone in my life as special as my great-grandmother. She called me Ellie and when she would see me, even when she was balancing herself on her walker, she would grab me with both arms and pull me into her ample bosom. "Oh, Ellie, how I've missed you!" she would say while holding me tight and rocking me back and forth. With Grandma Lyons there was never any doubt you were loved, never any doubt that you were worthy, never any doubt that at that moment, you were the most important thing in her world.

The honk of one of the pond ducks brought me back to reality. Why the memory of my great-grandmother invaded my thoughts at that moment, I had no idea. They say the sense of smell evokes memories more than the other senses. Perhaps that's true. Strange the way the brain works.

"Well, I guess we'd better check out the house. C'mon, girl." I directed Lilly to follow me up the porch steps. I opened one of the two screened double doors and located the security box containing the key fastened to the right door handle.

"Well, let's see what she looks like."

I punched in the code once again to a small box outside the door, gaining access to the keys. There were several keys on a small key ring, and it took me a few tries to figure out which one opened the front doors. Finally, inserting the third key into the lock, I heard the tumblers connect with a click and slowly opened the door. Lilly bounded in, practically knocking me over. I immediately let her off the leash, hoping she wouldn't scratch the polished hardwood floors. Suddenly remembering my instructions to turn off the alarm, I quickly located the alarm system in the foyer and deactivated it. I took a deep breath and turned around. Standing with leash in hand, I soaked in the house's interior. The foyer was well lit, even for this time of day and with no apparent lights on. I realized the source of light was streaming through the hallway and from the windows that were located at the back of the house. Standing in the center of the foyer was a large mahogany table displaying a crystal vase, almost certainly Waterford, containing at least two dozen fresh-cut lilies of the valley. Suspended from a twenty-foot or higher ceiling and directly above the table was an immense antique, white, wrought iron and glass chandelier. The staircase was the real stunner, positioned at the far end of the foyer in ninety-degree angles and running across the entire length of the second floor. Though the house most likely had been built in the early twentieth century and the woodwork at one time was almost definitely in dark wood, it was now painted a creamy white that made it look fresh with an understated elegance. To the right and left of the foyer were impressive arched doorways. Turn right and you enter a spacious living room in shades of green and gold. To the left, a dining room. A long table that could easily seat fifteen people took center stage. The room was equipped with floor-to-ceiling built-ins with a long buffet and china cabinet. It was all so much to take in. A completely furnished piece of heaven, and someone had given it to me. *Why on earth?* I wondered, shaking my head.

I felt Lilly's nose on my hand. She had already sniffed her way through the entire first floor.

"Well, don't just stand there, show me the rest," I commanded her. "C'mon, lead the way."

We walked past the stairway, through the arched hallway. A powder room was on the right. I marveled at the craftsmanship of the home. I couldn't begin to put a price tag on the cost of building a house like this today. We entered the back of the house, and I truly didn't think I could get any more surprised. I was wrong. A wall of windows spanned the entire back of the house. It was obvious that this part of the house had undergone some major remodeling. It was one of the largest and most inviting spaces I had ever seen, an open floor plan combining a gourmet kitchen and a family room. Though the room was huge, it had been designed with peace and tranquility in mind. A comfortable sectional in a shade of taupe faced a toffee-colored creek stone fireplace. Above the fireplace's mantel hung a glorious painting of the ocean, waves crashing upon the shore. The painting was both intense and serene, with vivid shades of blues and grays. And just to the right of the fireplace stood a baby-grand piano, positioned so that when playing, there was a perfect view of the river. French doors led to a stoned patio. The kitchen, well, it was so inviting that it made me want to roll up my sleeves and practice my culinary skills. Maybe not right now, but possibly in the next few days, after a trip to the store.

On the far wall was a delightful breakfast nook with a lovely view of the side garden, a perfect spot for morning coffee. At the kitchen's back end was a large walk-in pantry. I entered. There were mostly just cleaning and paper products on the shelves. Obviously, it had been cleaned out awhile back. But what really caught my attention was a door. It was bolted from the outside. I stared at it for a few seconds, then got up the courage to unbolt it and take a peek inside. Immediately, I was met with musty cool air. I flicked on the light switch just inside the door that illuminated a set of stone steps. I swallowed hard and, with much trepidation, made my way down, holding tightly to the bannister. I stopped halfway, too chicken to go any further. I knelt down to have a look. I laughed at my childish fear. It was a root cellar or had been at one time. It made sense, but I had seen enough. I went back up the stairs and bolted the door.

I returned to the den. I unlocked the French doors and walked out to the patio. The view was remarkable, the house itself was remarkable, but it was the grounds of this place that truly made it spectacular. This place, every inch, was a work of art.

Who are you, Mrs. Caldwell? Why in the world would you want me to have this? I am not worthy of such a gift. I don't know where the tears came from. There was no one there to hear me, but I still threw my hand over my mouth to stop a sob. I sat on the stone steps. The tears stung my eyes. I fought them hard, wiping them away. *I will not cry. I will not!* I must have sat there for several minutes. Lilly knew something was wrong because she kept pawing at me, trying to comfort me. She was such a good dog; I got her as a puppy shortly after my father died. She's always been a great source of comfort and companionship. Funny how, for many of us, we relate better to animals than human beings.

My pocket began to vibrate as the familiar ring tone sounded. I used my sleeve to wipe my eyes. It was my daughter, Mia. She was now living in Boston, having spent the last few years in London, where she met her current boyfriend Ian. I've always been in awe of her. She's had no fear of traveling the world and experiencing new things. However, she was ready to move back to the States, but not Louisville. So, she found a job working for a small advertising agency, and Ian landed a job in sales for a tech company.

"Hi, there."

"Hi! Where are you, Mom? I just spoke to Dad, and he said you just decided to take off for a few days. He said you weren't sure when you'd be back."

"Mia, I've got to take care of a few things. I'll explain everything to you and you brother later. Your dad will be fine for a few days by himself. But everything's okay. I promise. I'm in Georgia."

"Georgia, what's in Georgia? You sound really strange. Dad sounded so sad, like he's lost or something."

Mia's always been close to her father. Mia and I have always had a great relationship too, but, since her high school years, she's had momentary anger issues with me or maybe a lifetime's collection of resentments. I'm sure it's typical mother/daughter stuff, but, like every family, we have our challenges. Mia was a delight from the moment I gave birth to her. She was a lovely little girl—happy, energetic, bright, and self-motivated. Her older brother, well, he should have come with his own set of instructions. He was, to say the least, a challenge—whip smart and always ten steps ahead. Our family didn't take many summer vacations. I didn't have to tell the kids that the thought of a family vacation made Dan's blood pressure skyrocket. They knew it. Dan hated traveling, hated the beach, hated it if I laughed too loud or drank too much. And, if I'm truly being honest, my biggest fear is the combination of Dan and Alex together. What would happen between the two of them if Alex went with us, or even worse, if he stayed behind? Alex is my first born and I love him as fiercely as any mother could, but I always felt that God gave me more kid than I was prepared to handle. So, when it came to family vacations, there was no good option except to stay put. I would never say that our family was just too fucked up to go on vacation. So, I didn't say anything and let Mia travel with families that actually enjoyed being together, taking holidays, being social. I made a choice to live like that. I didn't know any other way. I loved Dan, I loved our family, but we seemed to struggle as a unit. Today, I look back on those days and wish I could have talked to my younger self. Tell her that it would be okay. That my children would grow up to be beautiful, responsible adults and that families are not perfect, and we would survive. But over the years, I have grown very tired of feeling like I always fall short of meeting everyone else's needs. I am tired of the parental and spousal guilt. I am a tired mediator. I am plain tired. So, when I got the call about the estate, I felt something I hadn't felt in years. I felt excited.

"Honey, your dad is a grown man. We've been married over thirty years. He'll be fine, we'll be fine. Just give me a little time."

"Yeah, but should you leave him like that? You know he's facing that biopsy next month, and he's really anxious about it."

I took a deep breath. Bringing up the biopsy as a weapon only served to anger me, and I didn't want to go there with her. Dan's urologist wanted him to have a biopsy on his prostate. He's been dealing with high PSA numbers for a few years and had a biopsy several years ago, and an MRI last year hadn't detected anything. But this last blood test indicated the highest number yet, and his doctor felt another biopsy was necessary. They couldn't get him in any earlier than next month. He was nervous, sure; we both were. But we'd dealt with many obstacles in our marriage, and we knew we would deal with this one too. Going to Georgia wouldn't change anything.

"Mia, you know I love your father, and that I've always supported him and always will. Sitting around each night worrying for a month waiting for the biopsy isn't helping his situation. There are times when you have to decide to carry on, and that's what we're doing. I'm not being insensitive. We're choosing to live our lives."

There was silence on the other end. I could almost feel her resentment coming through the phone.

"I still don't understand what you're doing and why you're in Georgia. Have you told Alex you're out of town?"

"No."

"Why not?"

"Because I chose not to."

"Did you tell Alex about Dad?"

"Yes."

"I don't get this. Why are you keeping secrets?"

"Because they're my secrets to keep, and I'll decide if and when I'll share them."

I really didn't know why I felt the need to keep all of this between me and Dan, but I did. I had asked him to keep the news of the estate to himself until I could make sense of it. I would trust my own instincts on this one.

"Fine. I just hope Dad's okay, that's all."

"Your Dad will be fine," I stated flatly. I didn't want to fight. I was tired.

"Hope so. I gotta go," she said.

"Okay, bye. Love you." But she had already hung up. I turned off my phone and put it in my pocket. I was done talking for the night.

"Alright, lady, let's finish our tour and get stuff out of the car." Lilly presented me with her paw and I gladly took it, wrapping my arms around her and burying my face in her fur. "Thanks, girl, I needed that," I said, laying my cheek against her soft fur. "Let's go."

I pulled myself up and quickly made my way back to the foyer. The upstairs would be next. The stairs were grand and the landing leading to the upstairs was spacious. A long foyer table flanked the inner wall. A lead glass mirror hung above with hurricane lighting sconces on each side of the mirror. Fresh-cut orchids had been placed in an azure porcelain vase and were sitting on the table. The reflection from the mirror made the flowers look twice their size. We began the tour. We went room by room, marveling at the attention to detail in each bedroom, all spacious and tastefully furnished, yet lacking any real personality that I could tell. However, the bedroom we entered on the west side of the house had a definite presence about it. I just knew this had to be Mrs. Caldwell's room. Soft, evening light was filtering through the tall windows. The room was a wash of soft greens, pinks, and browns. There was a melancholy feel to the room, even though it would have appeared quite lovely in one of those magazines that feature elegant southern homes. Thoughts of my own attempt at redecorating our bedroom came to mind. I was going for a coastal retreat, but instead got eclectic meets funeral home. I grinned thinking of Sharon's comments to me at the unveiling, "It's pretty, but not in a good way." However, whomever decorated this room did a much better job than I would have. A large sleigh bed was positioned on the short wall with a rosy-pink silk spread and a large cedar chest at its foot. A bedside table held a picture of a striking older woman in a silver frame. Though her face appeared rather youthful, her hair was almost white, one of those unique people whose hair grays prematurely. There was something oddly familiar about her. Something in her dark eyes. I picked up the picture and held it close, giving it a good look. Nope. Nothing. I couldn't place her. I set it back down and studied the rest of the room. A couch covered in a soft sable-colored fabric faced the fireplace with two wingback sage green chairs on either side of the fireplace. It was a comfortable room. Persian rugs decorated the floors. Arched bookshelves filled with books stood on either side of the fireplace. I let my fingers brush the spines. There were classics such as Hemingway's *The Old Man and the Sea*, Steinbeck's *Of Mice and Men*, Tolstoy's *War and Peace*, and Shelley's *Frankenstein* to name a few. There was also what looked to be entire collections of current authors such as Grisham, Patterson, Steele, Picoult, and even Koontz. Both bookshelves were completely stocked. Someone really loved their books. I could picture the lady in the photo, kicking off her shoes, curling up on the coach, and being completely transported to another place and time. I loved books. Remembering when my love affair with the written word began, I studied each volume. And I thought about how my sister cared little for reading. When Sharon asked me that day in Savannah about my sister, I began by saying, "She's nothing like me."

Four

"Ellen! Mom wants you in the house! *Now!*" she yelled.

I didn't answer. I didn't want to go back into the house and listen to the wailing of my baby brother, once again left in the playpen for far too long. Sitting cross-legged with my back against the house was my hiding spot. I usually shimmied to the top branch of our oak tree located in our front yard, but not today. Instead, I chose to escape to the far corner of our faded whitewashed clapboard house built on a concrete slab, engrossed in my latest Nancy Drew mystery, *The Hidden Staircase*. I had discovered the entire series while visiting the house of one of my parents' friends. The lady of the house found me in her back room, ogling all the books. She reached up and handed me two: "Here, Ellen, these can get you started, then just come back when you're finished with those and get more." And that's what I did to escape the reality of my world.

"There you are! Why didn't you answer me?" Jenny said, plopping down on the grass next to me.

"Didn't want to. I'm reading!" I replied without looking up.

"That's all you do. How can you just sit there and read? Ugh! That's got to be so boring. Mom wants you to come in and finish your chores. She's giving Jack his medicine, and she said he's having a bad morning. Aunt June's coming over with Charlie later and she wants you to vacuum."

Aunt June, I really loved her. My mom's younger sister was a constant around our house. Mom was almost nine years older than June, so she seemed like more of a big sister to us. I always got a lump in my throat when Charlie's name was mentioned. He was real sick. Mom said he had leukemia, and he probably wouldn't make it to Christmas. I loved Charlie; he was such a sweet, blond-haired, blue-eyed three-year-old. He loved being read to and always wanted me to sing his favorite song, "Puff, the Magic Dragon." He used to be hell on wheels, running and laughing and always into something. That changed. He was so sick he would just lay on the coach. He always asked me to tickle his face. Our older brother Jack was really sick too. Born with what Mom said were congenital deformities and kidney problems. Jack attended a special school for kids with orthopedic disabilities and other health issues. On days he wasn't feeling his best, Mom would keep him home. Jack was out of school more than he was in school. Mom and Aunt June were both fighting to keep their first-born sons alive. I hated living in that house. There was always so much fear, so much sadness, so much waiting for death.

"Do you think Charlie's going to die?" I asked.

"Yeah, Mom said he's real sick. Aunt June's been crying a lot lately," Jenny said.

"And Jack, you think he's going to die too?"

"Heck, I don't know! All I know is Mom said to come in and do your chores. NOW!"

My older sister was so bossy. She was fearless, afraid of nothing. She was a ten-year-old who could stare down both God and the devil at the same time. Jenny would challenge adults, whether it was our parents, others' parents, teachers, principals, or kids. It didn't matter. If she felt wronged, or simply wanted her way and felt justified in her beliefs, watch out. She wasn't a bully—well, she could be. She just didn't believe in taking no for an answer or putting up with what she considered nonsense. So, she fought, not so much physically—although she did her share of that— mostly, she knew how to strike someone's emotional Achilles heel. She had a sharp tongue, mean as a snake. She knew how to hurt. And she was my best friend!

That morning, the temperature already reached the low nineties. It was going to be a hot, sticky day. My eight, almost nine-year-old nostrils were picking up the smells of clover and wild onions. The world was buzzing from a lonely bumblebee making its way from one bloom to the next, gliding to the rhythmic *clip, clip, clip* of Mr. Benson's push mower next door. It was already too hot for early summer. I sat wondering if time could stand still, feeling the dampness of the morning grass seep through my shorts. I didn't want to leave my sanctuary or the wonderful mystery I was trying to help Nancy Drew and the girls solve. I sighed, knowing it was futile to ignore my mother's request. I stood up and brushed off the wet blades of grass from my seat and made my way to the front of my house. I was tempted to stall a moment longer and shimmy up our oak tree that stood in the front of our yard, but something caught my eye.

The curtains of the Jamesons' place from across the cul-de-sac seemed to move ever so slightly. I wasn't sure if there was anyone behind those curtains, but I got a strange feeling that we were being watched. I turned as fast as my Keds could carry me and yelled back to Jenny, "Last one to the front porch is a rotten egg!"

Five

"Holy cow! What made me flash back to that space and time?" I asked Lilly. She gave me her best blank stare and pant.

"You're a great conversationalist, girl," I laughed. "Come on, let's finish our tour and get stuff out of the car. I could use a bath and there's a bottle of wine icing in the cooler that's calling to me."

The house was truly enchanting. It dripped of charm and genteel elegance. Not exactly my decorating style, but lovely just the same. The second floor housed three other bedrooms, one that was extremely large and located at the back side of the house. This room looked as if it could have been easily transformed into a nursery or sitting room. It was bright and spacious, lodging large, tropical-looking plants, resembling prehistoric ferns that bent toward the light. A clear view of the water from the shoreline could be seen from this room.

"This room is great! So much light and a picture-perfect view. What do you think?" I asked Lilly who gave me a solitary woof.

"Oh! You like it too! Looks like maybe we'll have to flip a coin to see who gets ownership." I laughed. "C'mon, girl, it's time to wash up, get the car unpacked, and find something to eat. I know you're hungry."

In fact, a little something to eat wasn't such a bad idea. The granola bar and bottle of Diet Pepsi had worn off a long time ago. I was ready for a proper sandwich and an adult beverage. But first the car and then a shower to wash the remnants of the ten-hour car ride down the drain.

Lilly beat me to the front door. I attached the leash to her collar. I thought she would most likely stay with me, but I didn't want to chance it. The last thing I needed was to lose her. She definitely was my therapist, and good therapists are hard to find. Long walks, chasing water bottles, and nighttime cuddles have helped me through the rough patches of healing since my father's death, among other difficult family events.

With the leash in one hand, I managed in two trips to drag in a large suitcase, an overnight bag, a cooler, and my ever-so-faithful picnic basket that I've owned and used since the kids were little. It traveled with us on those very rare family outings, which might explain why it still looked so gently used. I unleashed

Lilly, grabbed the cooler, stacked the picnic basket on top, and made my way to the kitchen without dropping them.

After feeding Lilly, I decided a sponge bath in the downstairs powder room would have to do. I was just too tired to go upstairs and find a proper shower. I would take one tomorrow and wash my hair. I scrubbed and dried my face and hands quickly and changed into clean sweats and a t-shirt. Returning to the kitchen, I unpacked the picnic basket, made myself a substantial turkey sandwich, and grabbed the bottle of Pinot Grigio from the cooler. Doing my balancing act, I opened the French doors leading out to the patio and managed to park my full plate and the bottle of wine on the side table near the closest lounge chair. Making myself comfortable, I poured a very generous amount of vino into my plastic cup, closed my eyes, and sipped. *I must be in a dream, lounging here in this place, the kind of place I'd only seen on television. Who lives like this?* Obviously, Madeline and Anderson Caldwell did. Such a big place for only two people. And then, how many years did her lawyer say she lived here after the judge died? Ten or so? I looked out over the patio's stone wall and took in the view. The Georgia day was just on the cusp of passing the baton to the Georgia night. I could still make out the curve of the land, the outlines of the treetops, while listening to the sounds of nature's orchestra. It's paradise. But to live alone, no children, no grandchildren? Strange. Then, for whatever reason, my thoughts once again turned to my sister. No children, no grandchildren. My eyes grew heavy, and I couldn't resist closing them.

Six

1963

"Race ya to the playground!" she challenged me. We ran past the open screen door and headed for the carport to get our bikes.

I hopped on my lime green Schwinn bike with the ribbed banana seat and raced down Bakers Court toward the school playground as fast as my scrawny legs could go. My calves were burning, along with my lungs when I jumped off the bike and ran for the pavilion that we always tagged as home base. We were shoulder to shoulder when she reached out and shoved me sideways. I began falling, skinning the palms of my hands once impact came.

"That's not fair! I hate you!" I screamed.

She climbed on top of the center picnic table and raised both arms above her head, as if she had just won gold in the Olympics. "I win!" she laughed, throwing her head back while her waist-length blond ponytail swished back and forth.

"Yeah, but you cheated! I'm gonna tell Mom," I bellowed, knowing that I probably wouldn't.

We owned this playground. Well, not exactly, but we thought we did. It was the greatest playground a kid could have. It was not more than a three-minute bike ride from the house, down the road from the high school, and adjacent to our elementary school. I don't remember the playground ever having a name. We just called it "the playground." You could enjoy activities for a few weeks each summer provided by the community parks department. There would be baseball, baton lessons, hula hoop, and arts and crafts. I don't know how many God's eyes I made from twigs and yarn, but I'm fairly sure I could have opened my own God's eye store. This was the official gathering place for the neighborhood kids. The pavilion, a dark wooden octagon structure, provided shelter from the summer sun. Our imaginations would transform it to a witch's castle. You could climb her rafters and walk across her thirty-foot-high beams. We were lucky we didn't break our necks. We did manage a few splinters here and there. But we loved it. It was ours. It was a common getaway from the sadness that always seemed to encase our house. It was our safe place. And today, with no community park activities or anyone else, we had it all to ourselves.

Jenny jumped off the picnic table, totally ignoring me. I was sprawled on the grass where I had practically face-planted from her shove. She yelled, "Race you to the cactus!"

Balancing on my elbows, I watched her run toward the tall metal cactus that stood near the swings. She ran with her ponytail trailing behind. She wore a white cotton blouse with a Peter Pan collar and a pair of navy pedal pushers. Her lean body scurried up the cactus and perched on the third arm of the branch, or whatever you'd call that thing sticking out from a cactus. I always thought it was kind of a dumb piece of equipment. To me it was just this stupid-looking cactus, the color of Gumby with six slightly curved arms reaching skyward. At the end of each arm sat a flat, circular platform the size of a sandwich plate. You could climb up and sit on top of each arm. Sometimes a group of us would climb up, balancing our boney butts on the metal stem. There we'd sing, chant, or just talk until our fannies grew numb.

I picked myself up, wiping my scuffed palms on my cutoffs and walked over and looked up at Jenny.

"You didn't have to push me," I repeated.

"Sorry, didn't mean for you to fall."

"Yes, you did!"

Climbing up the second arm of the cactus, I positioned myself directly across from where Jenny was perched. I plopped down and glared at her. Getting no reaction, I finally gave up my ineffective death stare and glanced toward our elementary school, Frazier Heights, where, that fall, Jenny would start fifth grade and I would start fourth.

"I wonder if I'll get Mrs. Stopher this year. I hear she's mean, and she does something weird with her nose," Jenny said.

"I'm hoping I get Miss Dawson, she's young and real pretty."

Jenny and I were eighteen months apart, but only a grade apart. In our time at Frazier Heights, we never had the same teachers, except in kindergarten, and we both loved Mrs. Fields. She was everyone's favorite grandma!

"I loved Miss Crane last year. She always let me stay after school and clean the board erasers," I said.

"That doesn't sound like fun, you dope! She was getting you to do her work for her," Jenny chided.

"No, she wasn't. I liked staying after school and running through the halls when everybody was gone. It's kind of neat, and, you know, I didn't have to go straight home," I added.

Frazier Heights was probably built in the 1930s. It reigned supreme on Frazier Avenue and was a three-story dark brown brick structure with a basement. Anytime you entered the large double doors of the building and passed through the entryway, you could smell the rich aroma of wood, mingled with the enticing smells of baked rolls and chili. Add in the powerful wax solution used on the granite floors, and you had the bouquet of Frazier.

Each classroom had a see-through glass cloakroom with a gazillion brass hooks for coats and hats and built-in shelves for lunchboxes and other paraphernalia. Huge windows ran along the back of each room with those old shades attached, the kind that would fly up and out of reach if you let go the lever too quickly. The doors and stair railings were mahogany, and the classroom doorknobs were like large cut diamonds. Under each doorknob, there was a keyhole made of brass. I often wondered how many keys there were for the building and where they were kept. Most likely, they were in the principal's office. Miss Montgomery, our principal, was what people would refer to as an "old maid." She never married, and I could understand why. She was a little woman, no more than five feet tall with raven hair. She had a natural widow's peak (at least that's what my Grandma Lyons used to call it when your hairline forms a V in the middle of your forehead). Her appearance was made even more severe by the tight bun she wore at the nape of her neck. Her high-collared starched blouse, dark no-shaped mid-calf skirt, and black saddle shoes didn't help soften her appearance. She was a tiny woman, but you never wanted to be called to her office, for anything. Though Jenny was called quite often. Jenny's mouth and continuous resistance to authority made her a frequent visitor to Miss Montgomery's office. Yet, Miss M. really didn't scare Jenny. I don't think much did.

I loved school though. I loved the building, the teachers, the students, everything. I loved it because I wasn't home and just about any place was better than home.

"You wanna go see if Brenda Jean's home?" I asked.

Brenda Jean was one of three children in the Bishop family. Mrs. Bishop was a sweet lady with a round, pretty face. I never saw her without an apron tied around her thick waist. She had the greatest laugh. Mr. Bishop was kind of a muscular guy, completely bow-legged, and bald as an eagle. He was always wearing a white t-shirt two sizes two small, Bermuda shorts, and white socks up to his knees. His brown work boots completed his look. Mr. and Mrs. Bishop really liked to kid each other. She was always cracking jokes about his balding head. She said she got headaches from having to squint so much due to the shine that radiated off his forehead. Mr. Bishop called her Aunt Bee, because of her size, I guess. He said he liked his women like his muffins, sweet and plump. Then there's Brenda Jean, she was as about as skinny as a straw. The only thing skinnier than her body was her hair. She had the thinnest, straightest hair of anybody on the planet. If you drew a stick person and asked anybody who it was, they'd say Brenda Jean. I kid you not! The Bishops lived in one of the houses that backed up to the playground. Sometimes, when the Bishops' back gate was open, we could cut through their yard to go back home.

"I don't think she's home. She said something yesterday about having to go with her mom to get school shoes."

"I don't remember her saying that."

"Well, that's what she told me."

I was about to say something about how Brenda Jean was more my friend than hers, just to be mean, when

I noticed a boy on a bike riding down the sidewalk, coming from the direction of the high school toward us.

"Who's that?" I asked, sitting up a bit straighter on my perch.

"I dunno. I've never seen him before. He looks older."

He was maybe seventeen or eighteen, average height, with really dark hair. He had on a gray zipped jacket and blue jeans. I thought that was rather odd because it was late August, way too hot to be wearing those clothes. Not only did his clothes seem odd, but just something about him seemed kind of strange. My stomach tightened a bit, and it felt like an electrical current went up my spine.

He steered his bike off the sidewalk and began heading toward the pavilion, never taking his eyes off us. We watched him circle the pavilion. One, two, three, four times around he went.

"Do you think we'd better get out of here? Something doesn't feel right. I don't know what this guy's up to, and I'm not gonna stick around to find out," I stammered.

Before I could hop down, his bike made a beeline for the cactus, peddling as fast as he could, then coming to an abrupt skidding stop at the base of the cactus.

"Hey," he said.

"Hey," Jenny and I said in doubtful unison.

We were already standing up, ready to bolt.

"You gals haven't seen a stray dog around here, have you? Black and white, about this big," he said, holding his hands apart to indicate the relative size of the dog.

"Nope, we haven't seen a dog," Jenny replied.

"You sure?" he asked.

"I think we'd remember if we saw a dog," Jenny said, challenging his stupid repeated question.

"Okay, okay," he said with a smile. "I believe you. Man, it's too hot for this jacket," and he pulled off his jacket and laid it across his lap. "You girls live around here? Maybe if you live close by you might see him around and you can hold onto him for me. He got out of the gate a few hours ago. His name's Chief, like Chief Illini."

"Yeah," I said. Everyone knew Chief Illini, the mascot for the University of Illinois fighting Illini.

"We don't live around here…. We're just visiting a friend," Jenny lied. "She and her mom and dad are supposed to meet us here any minute."

"Oh yeah, where's your friend? I don't see your friend or her parents," he said looking around.

It was at that moment that I noticed his left hand had disappeared under his jacket.

"I just told you they're coming, but they're late, so we better just go."

"What's your rush?"

His left hand, no longer concealed by the jacket, was firmly gripping his penis. I looked away, then looked back at his face. His eyes were smiling. His mouth turned up with just the hint of a grin. I was sickened by the apparent satisfaction he was getting from exposing himself to us. I looked over at Jenny. She was seeing what I was seeing.

"RUN, RUN!" she screamed. She grabbed my hand and yanked me to the ground. When we hit the grass, she let me go and pure adrenaline took over. My heart was beating so fast I thought it might explode. We ran for our bikes that we'd left abandoned near the pavilion. I could feel him behind me.

"Leave us alone, and your dick's really tiny!" she shrieked.

Oh, dear God, why'd she have to go and scream that? Now he's really going to be pissed, I thought, and I choked out a laugh at what I thought was kind of silly thing for me to think given the circumstances.

Of course, Jenny reached her bike first, "Hurry! he's right behind you!"

I managed to pick up my bike, running with it at first, until I was able to lift my body onto the seat and my feet found the pedals.

"Hurry, head for the Bishops!" she screamed.

"I'm behind you! Hurry!"

For a split second I lost control of the bike. It began to wobble and dip. Somehow, I straightened it, keeping myself from spinning out of control. His front wheel bumped against my back wheel.

"C'mon, bitches, I'll show how big my dick is!" he screeched.

I could see Jenny had reached the Bishops' back gate. Jumping off the bike, she ran frantically and pulled at the gate latch.

"Help, help!" she screamed. She fumbled with the latch and finally flung the gate open, running into the Bishops' back yard. I jumped off my bike and flew as fast as my legs could carry me.

"What's all the ruckus?" I heard a familiar man's voice ask.

Mr. Bishop was coming out of his garage, wiping grease from his hands on a towel.

"That guy's chasing us!" Jenny screamed, pointing in the direction of the boy.

All three of us watched as the boy came to a complete halt just a few feet from the fence. Once he saw Mr. Bishop, he turned his bike around and shot down the sidewalk. I suddenly felt the hot liquid trickle down my leg. Oh my God, I had just peed in my pants. I could feel the warmth spread between my legs and seep into my cutoffs. I didn't know if I was more scared of what just happened, or the fact that I just wet myself. It didn't really matter, neither Jenny nor Mr. Bishop seemed to notice.

Seven

A wet fog woke me. I sat up startled and disoriented. The glass of wine in my hand had only a few drops left with most of the contents soaked into my pants. Lilly jumped up as well—I startled her. The sky was black velvet and there appeared to be thousands of stars above. Good heavens, what time is it? I reached for my phone. It indicated 1:29 a.m., and I had apparently missed two calls from Dan. I sat up and rubbed my eyes. It was way too late to try and call him. I didn't have the energy or desire to have a conversation now. I was just too tired. He would be asleep anyway. I quickly texted him, letting him know I was fine, that I had fallen asleep, and I'd call him in the morning. I got up, picked up the almost empty bottle, my glass, and my plate and carried them into the house. Lilly followed me in, leash dragging behind her. I dumped everything on the counter and eyed the couch in the family room.

"Why not?" I said. I felt strange in this place and finding a room to sleep in just seemed creepy at that moment. Grabbing my suitcase from the foyer, I brought it into the den and found the articles I needed. Next, a trip to the bathroom. I quickly peeled off my wet sweats and, once again, washed off the best I could and changed into my long, red, University of Louisville t-shirt. Fancy sleepwear was never my style. I quickly brushed my teeth, flossed, and went back to the family room. Finding a soft gray-blue afghan and the sofa's throw pillows, I settled in and motioned for Lilly to join me. She plopped down next to me, placing her head over my legs. I stroked her head and thought about where I was and what I was doing here.

"Well, girl, here we are. Why, I have no idea, but we're going to find out, aren't we?"

I didn't know if I was being selfish. Maybe Mia was right. I wasn't really thinking about Dan. I was thinking about me. Should I feel guilty? Here we go again, my guilty brain on the hamster wheel. I shut my eyes tight and willed my brain to stop tumbling. I'm here now. This is where I need to be. *Stop it! Stop it! Stop it! Live in the moment.* I inhaled, held my breath, counted to three, then slowly exhaled. I repeated the exercise three more times, willing my mind and body to find inner calm. I could feel myself relaxing, and, before long, I gave in to my body's need for peace.

"Tomorrow," I murmured to Lilly, "I'll think about things tomorrow."

The sound of my ringtone woke me up. Natural light was flooding through the French doors, forcing me to open one eye and peer through the morning muddle. Kicking the afghan off, I followed the sound. I had plugged the phone in and left it on the kitchen counter shortly before crashing on the coach, but everything was still a blur. I found the phone. It was Dan.

"Hi there," I said yawning and rubbing my eyes.

"Did I wake you?

"Yeah, but that's okay, I needed to get up."

"I know, I'm sorry. I got in and got a little distracted. I was so tired I sat down in a chaise on the patio and fell asleep. When I woke up, it was just too late to call you. It was a long day and I guess I was a bit overwhelmed by everything."

"I understand. So, what's it like?" he asked.

"You wouldn't believe this place. It's really extraordinary! It's probably one of the most charming homes I've ever seen. If I owned this place, I certainly wouldn't have given it to a total stranger, that's for sure."

Laughing out loud Dan said, "You *do* own that place."

"On paper I guess, but it just doesn't seem right. I'm going to do some more exploring today, then I have an appointment at three with Mrs. Caldwell's attorney. Maybe I'll learn more after speaking with him."

"Well, keep me posted. You know, I could come so you don't have to be alone."

I let the silence linger a bit before answering.

"I know, and I appreciate it. But, like I said before, I think I need some time. All this just came at a time when I think I needed a little diversion from, well, I don't know for sure, my own thoughts maybe. I've just been a bit confused lately."

"You know I love you," he said.

"I know. I love you too. It's just, well, I'm at a place in my life that I need to take a step back and take some time for me. You and the kids are my entire life, and I'm so grateful for all of you, but…."

"I get it," he interrupted, "or at least I think I do."

"Just be patient, Dan."

"I'll try. Listen, I've got to go, I'm being paged over the intercom. I had to come in early with an issue in the shop. Call me later, okay? Let me know how the lawyer thing goes."

"Will do. Love you."

"Love you, too. Bye."

A shadow of guilt cast upon me as I hung up the phone. Maybe I should have asked him to come with me, but I really had a strong urge to do this on my own, and, for once, I did what I wanted to do. So, I shook off the guilt and went about the task of facing the day. I decided this morning would be a good time to do a little exploring, but first, coffee, maybe a banana muffin from the stash of food items I'd brought with me, and then a real shower. I was so thankful there was a working coffeemaker. Next to it stood a white porcelain cannister of coffee beans and a coffee grinder. *Yeah!* I brewed a pot. It took all of two minutes to devour my muffin and wash it down with a cup of strong black coffee. I quickly brushed the crumbs from my face and hands, refilled my mug, and retrieved my suitcase. I then made my way upstairs in search of a working shower. While exploring yesterday, I knew there was a bathroom off of what I could only assume was Mrs. Caldwell's bedroom. I was told that the estate would continue to keep the water and electricity going until the new owner transferred it to their name. They also secured a cleaning service and there was a property manager who took care of other details. I would probably find out more about that this afternoon when I met with Mrs. Caldwell's lawyer. I entered the bathroom carrying my bag of toiletries, makeup necessities, and my outfit for the day. I dumped my cargo on top of the vanity and surveyed the area. It was impressive. There was a large claw tub, a separate shower, double vanities, white marble countertops and floor, a separate water closet, and a fully stocked linen closet. It was very feminine with its brushed nickel hardware and rose-and-dove-grey hand towels. Small, lavender-scented soaps were arranged in duplicate porcelain soap dishes. All of it was almost too pretty to use, but I needed a shower. I looked at the pile of stuff I had just dumped on the "too pretty" countertop and inwardly apologized to Mrs. Caldwell for being a bit of a mess. Tidy wouldn't exactly describe me. It took a few minutes to figure out how to work the shower and adjust it to the temperature I needed. I stepped in and let the hot water wash away the remnants of the last twenty-four hours. It felt amazing. I stayed in probably longer than I should have, using way too much shampoo and the coconut body wash I brought along and I loved. I finally made myself get out. I decided to forgo the hairdryer and just towel-dry my wet mop. I threw on a pair of khakis, a white t-shirt with a tiny bumble bee on the left breast pocket, and the word *buzz* written in cursive trailing behind the bee. I completed the outfit, shoving my feet into a pair of plain white sneakers. I was ready to face the day.

I started by rummaging through drawers, hoping to find anything that might give me a clue as to the identity of this lady. Beginning with the bedside tables in her bedroom, I found mostly items of little help. There was a pair of reading glasses, unused stationery, long-kept birthday cards from friends or family members. None of the envelopes were with the cards, no one wrote a lengthy note that would give me some sort of clue as to whom I might speak with. There were bookmarks, a *Southern Living* magazine, 2017 Christmas edition, several hairpins, and a small bottle of hand lotion. Nothing that you wouldn't find in countless bedside tables. I moved on to the cedar chest located at the foot of the bed. Opening it almost brought tears to my eyes as my nostrils received the pungent sent of cedar, mixed with something floral. It took me a second to focus my watery eyes, but when I did, I felt as if I had just invaded a very private space.

Wrapped in heavy plastic was what appeared to be ivory silk, possibly discolored over time. It looked to be her wedding gown. I took the wrapped garment out of the chest and placed it on the floor. Under the gown rested a crinoline veil and a pair of what were once white satin shoes. I picked up the shoes, size six. She was a petite woman. Next was a white Bible with the name *Madeline Marie Caldwell* embossed in gold on the cover. A silver cross on a chain was nestled in a page of an underlined passage from Isaiah 57:15. The passage itself referred to something about "broken hearts being revitalized." It meant nothing to me. I opened the front of the Bible and saw in bold script handwriting, the following note:

To My Darling Del,

May God watch over you and forever keep you safe.

All my love,

Anderson

He called her Del. I got a lump in my throat. He must have loved her very much. *Well, here's the beginning of learning who these people were.* Reaching into the chest to investigate a few more items, I was stopped by the sound of a buzzer. I sat up, waiting to hear if the sound would present itself again. Sure enough, the harsh *buzz* sounded once again and then I heard Lilly barking. I jumped up, quickly put the items back in the chest, and went to find the source of the interruption.

For the third time the buzzer sounded. It was coming from the intercom at the front door. I looked at my watch, it wasn't even 10:00 a.m. Who in the world would be stopping by this morning? I pressed the button.

"Hello?" I said.

"Hello, yes, sorry to bother you. Am I speaking to Ellen Williams?"

"Um, yes, and who am I speaking with?" I answered reluctantly.

"Hi there, I'm Hunter McGaffey, Madeline Caldwell's nephew. I was wondering if I might have a moment of your time?"

"Uh, sure," I said hesitantly. "Let me see if I can locate the button that unlocks the gate."

"It should be just to the right of the intercom."

"Oh. I got it, is it opening?"

"Yep, that does it."

I punched in the code to deactivate the alarm and stepped out on the porch. Lilly came out to stand next to me. I petted her head as I waited for Hunter McGaffey. He was the doctor, the surgeon, I believed, that had been briefly mentioned by the lawyer. Was he coming to intimidate me? Was he angry? Did I just let a serial killer onto the grounds, and would it be weeks before anyone would find my remains in the duck pond?

"Oh, dear Lord, Ellen," I said out loud to myself and Lilly. "Why do you always think the worst? Brace yourself, girl, because here he comes."

I could make out a white convertible coming around the bend of the pond. Even as nervous as I was to meet this guy, I also marveled at the seductiveness of the property. Goodness, I'll bet Madeline really loved this place.

In less than a minute, Hunter drove up in a gorgeous Mercedes convertible. He pulled up behind my X5, and I could see that he was a rather handsome fellow. I would guess him to be somewhere in his early forties. He was wearing aviator shades and had a thick head of wavy salt-and-pepper hair. Lilly and I made our way down the steps to meet him. He was tall, over six feet, wearing a blue sports jacket over a crisp white shirt opened at the collar, dark jeans, and loafers. He looked elegantly casual. The kind of guy you'd see in a Men's Wearhouse commercial or *GQ* magazine.

I watched as he got out of the car, removing his sunglasses and pocketing them in his jacket as he came toward me. Reaching out his hand to shake mine he said, "Hunter McGaffey. Thanks so much for seeing me without notice. I hope this isn't too much of an inconvenience. I was hoping to catch you before I went into the hospital this morning."

"Ellen Williams. No, not an inconvenience at all. And this is Lilly," I said.

"Nice to meet you, Lilly," he said, patting her head.

"Come on in, I have a pot a coffee on if you'd like a cup."

"That would be great."

I led him through the foyer and into to the kitchen. I was feeling rather awkward, this being a home he had spent his entire life in, and me waltzing him through as if he were the guest. But this is the situation I found myself in.

"Please, have a seat," I offered, motioning to the coach in the den. "How do you take your coffee?"

"Just black, thanks."

I retrieved two coffee cups and filled them. "So, you're a heart surgeon here in Brunswick?" I asked, handing him a cup of steaming coffee, then took the chair opposite Dr. McGaffey.

"Yes, I'm in cardiothoracic surgery."

"Wow, that's quite impressive. It must keep you extremely busy."

"That it does! Well, that and two teenage daughters."

"Oh, yeah," I said with a smile. "My husband and I managed to survive raising two teenagers. We have two adult children, Mia and Alex. Parenting's the hardest of all jobs, isn't it?"

"Yes, it's a challenge. They're terrific girls. They split their time between their mother and me. My ex-wife Beth is an internist living in Jacksonville."

"Gee, you are both doctors!"

"Yes, we met in medical school. Unfortunately, our

careers took their toll on the family, on our marriage," he said with a tinge of sadness. "Anyway, the girls are staying with me this summer. Claire just completed her freshman year at Emory, and Maggie's going to be a senior next year. Both are extremely ambitious young women. They've only been home for a couple of weeks, and I can't keep up with them."

"Sounds to me like they're a lot like their parents. You must be very proud of them."

"That I am."

There was a moment of awkward silence. I took a sip of my coffee before I dove into the conversation I knew was coming. Setting my coffee down and clearing my throat, I began

nervously.

"I know this is a rather odd situation we're finding ourselves in, but I want you to know that I'm as confused by this chain of events as you most likely are."

Without warning, Lilly hopped up on the couch, practically knocking over Dr. McGaffey's mug as she put her head in his lap.

"I am so sorry! Lilly! Get down!"

"No," he laughed, "she's fine, really."

"Sorry, she's eager to meet new people. The good news is that you get a free lint roller with every visit."

He smiled and said, "Don't worry about it."

"So, how can I help you? Or do you have information that could make sense of this for me?"

"No, I don't," he stated. "I really don't know. I'm at a loss as to why Aunt Del made the decisions she did."

"Del? Oh, that's right. I think I heard somewhere that she was called Del," I said feeling a bit guilty having just discovered that piece of information in her Bible inscription.

"Yes, that's what the family called her. My aunt, well, she was always a bit of a mystery to our family. I guess my question to you is, how did *you* know her?"

"Well, that's the thing, I didn't, or, at least, I don't think I did. This was as much a shock to me as I'm sure it was to your family. I'm totally baffled as to why she would leave a stranger her house. It really doesn't make sense. But according to her lawyer, this is what she wanted." Trying to explain the inexplicable to him began to make me even more nervous. I thought I'd keep the photographic proof from him for now. I didn't know him or his motives. He seemed like a really good guy, a caring nephew, but for all I knew, he could be inwardly seething at his aunt's decision to give away the family estate to a stranger. I imagined anyone would have been angry.

"So, I don't know why yet. But I'm here trying to find out. Obviously, there's a reason for all of this, and I can't help but feel that she wants me to know something. But, for the life of me, I don't know what it is. Believe me when I say that I'm not a person who would take something that doesn't belong to me. I've got my own family, a home, and a business in Louisville. This came as a total surprise to me, and I'm only here trying to figure out what she wants me to know. Once I'm able to do that, I may know what the next step will be. I know it might sound strange, but I feel an obligation to find out the truth. You said she was a mystery to your family. In what way?"

He cleared his throat and said, "Aunt Del was a reserved and private lady, but truly kind. However, there was no mistaking her inner strength. She and my uncle were married a bit later in life. According to my mother, her older brother, my uncle came back to Georgia after having practiced law in Chicago. It might have been in the mid-sixties, I think, and, when he came back, he brought with him a wife. The family was really surprised. My mother said that neither Uncle Anderson nor Aunt Del spoke of her past. Aunt Del was an orphan and an only child with no family to speak of. They had met by chance in a drugstore where Aunt Del was working. Uncle Anderson said he took one look at her behind the counter and fell in love. He used to say that the moment he saw her, he couldn't remember what he went into that drugstore for," he chuckled. "Anyway, he asked her out, she accepted, and the rest was history. Throughout their marriage they were extremely committed to one another. They never had children but opened up their home for holidays and family gatherings. They loved to entertain. We had lots of happy memories here, yet Aunt Del always seemed a bit sad."

"Sad in what way?" I asked.

He shrugged, "Oh, I don't know. You'd catch her watching the children run around, and she'd have this look about her. I remember once the family was gathered for a picnic on the Fourth of July. In the evening, we were setting off fireworks. I remember grabbing a handful of firecrackers and I was about to set them off, when one of the men at the picnic, an older gentleman, I can't even remember his name now, grabbed me by the collar and told me to stop. Aunt Del, without hesitation, told him to remove his hands from my collar. 'He's just a boy,' she said. For a moment, everyone stopped what they were doing. Then she just turned and walked away."

I tried to visualize this petite woman standing up for a young boy. It probably caught everyone off guard, if she was normally as reserved as described.

"Dr. McGaffey?"

"Please, call me Hunter," He replied.

"Okay. Hunter, can I ask you a personal question?"

"Sure."

"How angry are you right now at your aunt and at me, for that matter? Believe me, I understand if you are. Hell, I think I'd be really pissed off if my aunt left the family estate to a complete stranger. You know people murder people for a lot less," I laughed nervously.

He stared at his coffee for several seconds before answering. I could see he was struggling to formulate his answer.

"I'd be lying if I said I wasn't initially upset. I don't know why she did what she did. She was of sound mind when she made her last will and testament, and it was her property. She could do with it what she wanted. I just wish I understood her motives. Don't get me wrong, I don't need the money, nor does anyone else in the family. In fact, Uncle Anderson gifted us a rather sizeable sum prior to his death, and my girls and I received a generous amount from my aunt upon her death. So, it's not like we were jilted out of the family fortune or anything. But this house, this house was their jewel, their world. It meant everything to them. I just wanted to meet the person to whom my aunt left her most prized possession. I was hoping you might be able to shed some light on this."

"I wish I had some answers for you, I really do. I'm as much in the dark as you are. Again, I don't know why she left this to me. I didn't know your aunt. I didn't know your uncle. There is no connection whatsoever between your family and mine. I am here to find answers. Your aunt has bestowed on me this unbelievable gift. People don't do that. But she did it. And I am bound and determined to find out why. And when I do, I will know what I'm supposed to do."

"What you're supposed to do? What does that even mean?" he asked with a challenging edge to his voice. In that brief exchange, I knew that I was dealing with someone who was used to getting answers, and fast. His face grew dark.

"I don't know," I said, more defensively than I

intended. "We'll all just have to wait and see what develops."

Just as quickly as the change came over his face, so it disappeared. He abruptly stood up and brushed the dog hair from his jacket and jeans.

"I've taken up enough of your time. I've got to get going." Reaching into his coat pocket, he pulled out a card and handed it to me. "Here, if you do find out anything at all, please give me a call. It would be nice to know the why of all of this."

"Of course. I understand," I said.

I walked him to the door and watched him drive away. I had a feeling that before this was over, I'd be learning a lot more about Dr. McGaffey. Once again, as I gazed out, I found myself overwhelmed by it all. I wrapped my arms around myself, feeling the need to find comfort. It didn't work. I closed my eyes and took a deep breath. The warm morning air touched my face. I needed air. I needed to move. I needed a walk.

"C'mon, girl, let's go get your leash and do some outside exploring. Plenty of time to search the house later."

The click of Lilly's toenails on the hardwood as she followed me in search of the leash comforted me. The familiar sound of home. I grabbed my keys, retrieved my sunglasses from the bottom of my purse, and picked up the leash that I had left on the kitchen counter. I made a mental note to find a more sanitary spot in the future for her leash. I almost grabbed my phone, then decided to give myself a half hour of an information-free zone.

Okay, let's start out front," I commanded.

What was left of the morning was showing signs of becoming a scorcher of a day. The temperature was already in the high eighties with extreme humidity. My hair would probably resemble Harpo Marx by the end of this walk, but who cares? My meeting with the lawyer wasn't until later this afternoon, and I'd have plenty of time to clean up before I drove into town.

I made my way down the driveway, then followed a man-made path that led around the pond to the southwest side of the property. The grounds were lush with tall trees, ornamental grasses, and wildflowers. It became more untamed as we traveled down the path. Grasshoppers bounced out of the brush and kept Lilly entertained. We had walked no more than maybe an eighth of a mile down the footpath when we came to an area that seem to miraculously open to a grassy hillside. On top of the hill stood a large white gazebo trimmed in forest green. It was the kind of structure you'd see in movies, where the band would play while people sat on blankets, listening to a concert. I could picture that Fourth of July Hunter described. I would bet this is where most of the family's outside events took place. It was the perfect spot. Suddenly, a squirrel darted up a tree and Lilly practically pulled my arm out of its socket in pursuit. She came to an abrupt halt under an oak. I tugged on her leash but couldn't get her to budge. She tried jumping at first on her hind legs, her front paws resting on the tree trunk. When that didn't work, she began barking incessantly, and, when that didn't work, she sat down at the bottom of the tree and just stared up at the squirrel. I could almost hear the squirrel say to Lilly, "Well, what's your plan, dumbass?" As I stood there giving Lilly a few minutes to realize this was a game of futility, I was struck by the strong smell of honeysuckle. I looked around to see if I could identify where the scent was coming from. There it was. An old metal bird feeder, now with splotches of green patina, was practically hidden by overgrown shrubs that held a familiar climbing vine. Yes, it was most definitely honeysuckle. I knew that scent anywhere. Immediately, I was transported to another place and time.

Eight

1963

"Do you smell that?" Jenny asked as we made our way around a line of bushes. "It smells good."

"Yeah, that's honeysuckle," I stated proudly.

"How do you know?"

"'Cause Dad told me."

She didn't challenge my botanical knowledge and continued trudging forward. She was on a mission. "Let's cut through Miss Gallagher's backyard. We can reach the train tracks faster," Jenny said as she wove in between houses.

"Okay!"

"Here, this way. You gotta keep your mouth shut too, 'cause Mom thinks we're going to the playground."

"I'm not gonna say anything," I replied defensively.

"I got about five bucks in my pocket. I found most of it in the couch cushion, some in a Folger's can in the cabinet, and some loose change in Dad's car."

"You don't think they'll find out? That's stealing, you know?"

"For five bucks! Sometimes you're really stupid!"

"I'm not stupid."

"Yes, you are."

I stopped dead in my tracks behind Miss Gallagher's house and stomped my foot, "I'm not going if you're gonna call me names!"

She laughed and said, "Yes, you will, because you want to play putt-putt too. We've got enough money to get milkshakes at Top Boy after we play," she said.

"Hey girls, what are you doing back there?"

It was Dorothy Gallagher, standing on her back stoop, one hand displaying a smoldering cigarette while the other rested on her rail-thin hip.

"Nothing, Miss Gallagher, we're just cutting through," Jenny said.

"You girls shouldn't be cutting through back here."

"Why?" Jenny challenged.

"It's not safe to be so close to the tracks. It's not safe back behind these houses," she said, gesturing toward the houses that flanked the tracks. She pointed directly to old man Jameson's house. "Haven't your parents told you to stay away from the tracks?"

"No, and it's a free country," Jenny challenged defiantly.

I stood there like a scared rabbit. I was waiting to take my cue from my older sister, but I was smart enough to know that she didn't always make the best choices.

"Well, it might be a free country, but I'm telling you to stay clear of this side of the tracks. You can cut through your own backyard, anyway. Why come this way?"

"'Cause it's faster," Jenny stated.

Miss Gallagher was an odd duck. She was extremely tall for a woman, almost six feet. She was thin and completely flat-chested. Her hair was cut in a super-short pixie the color of straw with a reddish tint. She wore a permanent scowl on her face and always appeared to be in a bad mood. The boys in the neighborhood called her Dot the Dyke. I never knew what that meant. We usually just avoided her, but today we had failed at that task.

"We're not bothering anybody, Miss Gallagher, and we're leaving now," I said, finding my voice.

Jenny grabbed my hand and began running in the

direction Miss Gallagher had told us not to. I followed her as fast as I could go. We hopped the tracks and made it to the other side. We knew she wouldn't come after us. She just wanted us gone.

"Why's she gotta be so mean? We weren't doing anything!" I said between gasps of air.

"She's just a bitch," Jenny sneered.

"Yeah, she is."

We spent the next hour and a half playing putt-putt and ending our adventure with chocolate shakes so thick the straws stood up by themselves. With our stomachs full and the money gone, we made our way back, except this time we'd swing around the other direction to avoid Miss Gallagher.

Cutting back around the Jamesons' house and making our way to the cul-de-sac, we were spotted by old man Jameson as he swept his front porch. He was in pain with every sweep. Wearing his usual dungaree overalls and red plaid shirt, he resembled an old, bald farmer.

"Well, hello, ladies. How are you today?" he asked in a jovial voice.

"We're good, thanks! *Keep walking*," Jenny said in my ear.

"What've you two been up to?" he inquired.

"Nothing much," Jenny stated.

Just then, we could hear the squawk of the Jamesons'

mynah bird through the screen door.

"Shut up, Bird! Crazy bird, never knows when to hush," Mr. Jameson said as he continued to sweep.

"Can we see him?" I asked. Jenny jabbed me hard in the side with her elbow.

"No, we gotta go," she said through clenched teeth.

Ignoring her and rubbing my aching side, I made my way up the sidewalk to Mr. Jameson. I never passed up an opportunity to visit with an animal. Any animal.

"Why, sure you can. Come on in."

"Probably shouldn't," Jenny muttered.

"Oh, c'mon, this darn bird won't bite," Mr. Jameson said.

"I want to see him," I stated.

"Then come on in, little missy. I'll introduce you." Mr. Jameson opened the screen door wide to let us pass.

Though hesitant, Jenny followed. I absolutely adored all animals, large and small. My mom said that once the doctor's office called the house to make sure I was alright. We hadn't been to their office in several months for a dog bite, cat scratch, bee sting, or any other animal-related casualty.

I hadn't stepped more than a foot into the room when my nose wrinkled, and my eyes began to water. The powerful smell of pipe tobacco, fried onions, and moth balls filled my nostrils. It took a few seconds for my eyes to adjust, having left the bright summer light and entered a cavern. Two mismatched leather chairs sat almost in the center of the room with a large console television directly opposite for optimal viewing pleasure, or for an old man that couldn't see. An ancient lamp sat on a small table in between the chairs, and a pipe rested on a glass ashtray, which explained the intense tobacco smell. I knew Mr. Jameson lived with his grown son and his son's young wife, Mae. Dad said Henry had been in the Army and served in Korea. He looked to be a bit older than our dad. Rarely did you see him talking to anyone in the cul-de-sac. Neighbors gossiped from time to time about both Henry and his wife. He would on occasion wave in greeting, but that was about it. I once heard that Henry had picked up a puppy by the scruff of its neck and thrown it clear across the train tracks. I didn't know if that was true. I had seen him last winter assisting his aging father to and from the car when the snow and ice were heavy on the sidewalks. It was obvious he didn't want to socialize. So, everyone pretty much stayed clear of him. And, as far as his wife, well, rumor had it that she was nuts, completely off her rocker. She spent the majority of her time in some mental hospital outside of the city. Supposedly, she'd come home to visit, but there was no sign of either one of them today. However, there was an occupant present that was much more interesting to me. Displayed prominently, just to the left, and before you entered the kitchen, was a huge bird cage, housing one of the biggest birds I had ever seen. He had coal-black wings with an orangish-yellow beak and sharp talons clutching his perch. He quickly paced along his perch, bobbing his head up and down as he went. He shook one claw, then the other. He looked agitated.

"What's his name?" I asked.

"Well, we call him Bird."

"Bird," I repeated. "Why don't you give him a proper name?"

"Henry just calls him Bird, don't really know why," Mr. Jameson said, scratching the back of his bald head.

"Watch this!" He bent down next to the cage.

"Hello, Bird," he said.

"Hello, Henry," the bird sang out.

I jumped a foot hearing the bird speak.

"He can talk?" I asked in amazement.

Mr. Jameson laughed heartily and said, "Well, he can say a few things he's been taught. Watch this. Who's a pretty bird?"

"Bird's a pretty bird," sang out Bird.

"Now you try it."

I crouched down to Bird's eye level and timidly said, "Hello, Bird."

"Hello, Henry," the bird replied immediately. It actually sounded more like "*Ello, Enry.*"

"Oh, my God! Jenny, are you hearing this? He's amazing!" I cried.

"Yeah, amazing. Okay, we gotta go!"

"What else can he say?" I pleaded for more.

"Not really much else."

"Can we come back again and see him?"

"You can come anytime you'd like," Mr. Jameson said.

"Well, bye," Jenny said as she dragged me by the elbow.

"Bye, Mr. Jameson!" I hollered back as my sister pulled me through the yard.

"Get off me! Why are you pulling me?" I screamed.

"Stay away from that house! Don't go back there!" she said through clenched teeth.

"You can't tell me what to do!"

"Yes, I can! I'm telling you to stay away from those people and that stupid bird!"

Nine

The sound of birds chirping overhead interrupted my thoughts. Lilly was eager to keep moving. I glanced at my watch and didn't realize how much time had gotten away from me. "C'mon, lady, we need to head back!"

I'd have just enough time to make myself a bite to eat, clean up, and head into town. I was anxious to hear what this lawyer had to say.

Driving into town I was struck once again by the beauty of Brunswick, the Port City. It was a picture-perfect seaside postcard. Handsomely restored historic homes with their manicured lawns encased by ornate fences lined the streets. Churches stood tall and proud. Colorful storefront windows enticed visitors with antiques, novelty gifts by local artisans, and mouth-watering treats like homemade fudge, pies, and cakes. This was just the kind of town you'd want to explore with your girlfriends. Endless shopping and eating. Though a bit hot and muggy, I'd rather wander the streets of Brunswick than spend time in an attorney's office. However, I was here for a reason. Sightseeing would have to be put off for the moment. I located the building and pulled into a space right in front. Finding a parking space like that never happened at home. The glass front door read *Cameron, Carmichael, and Associates* in gold lettering, and each lawyer was listed below with their first initial and last name. I was obviously in the right place. As I pushed open the door and entered, a bell gently announced my arrival. Well, not specifically my arrival, but each visitor's arrival. The sound of the bell made me feel welcome and it strangely comforted me.

I stood in the vast entryway. In the center was an extremely large walnut table with a basket of fresh-cut chrysanthemums. Ornate flower arrangements appeared to be a common theme. The walls were papered a soft beige grass cloth, giving the room a tranquil effect. To the right was a vacant receptionist's desk with a computer. To the left were four comfy chairs upholstered in a cream-colored fabric surrounding a coffee table that displayed several popular magazines. The waiting areas was as empty as the receptionist's desk.

"Hello? Anyone here?" I asked. "Hello?"

I was about to make my way down the hall when a voice called out, "Be right with you."

Oops, maybe I caught the receptionist taking a potty break.

"So sorry to keep you waiting," said a bouncy lady with a head of platinum blond hair teased practically to the ceiling. She was wearing a pair of red-framed and rhinestone eye glasses, and a long red silk blouse covered in yellow, turquoise, and purple flowers over a pair of straight black slacks. Her beautifully polished red toenails were encased in three-inch strappy silver sandals.

"Can I help ya, sweetie?" she asked in a thick, southern drawl with a bright smile.

"Uh, yes, sorry," I said after losing my train of thought for a minute as I stared at this fascinating woman. "I'm Ellen Williams. I have an appointment to see Mr. Carmichael."

"Oh, yes, Ellen Williams. Well, hellooo, honey! It's so nice to meet ya! We've all just been dying to meet ya, you know, being the mystery lady and all. We all just loved Mrs. Caldwell. She was just the sweetest thing. Not like a lot of these country club prima donnas. She was kind and every inch a lady. She and the judge were really loved in this town. Oh, I'm sorry, I'm just babbling on. I'm Judy Cameron," she said, reaching out with both hands to take mine.

"Cameron, as in Cameron, Carmichael, and…?" I trailed off, trying to hide my surprise.

Her huge laugh was undeniably the most incredibly genuine thing I'd ever heard.

"Ha! Yep, that's me. Guilty as charged," she said still chuckling. "But don't you worry about being rather shocked, we get that all the time. Sometimes we get these big city lawyers comin' in here and acting like they're above it all. You know the type. One day a group of them came down from New York City to settle a land dispute. I ushered them into the conference room, and one of them said 'Dear, would you mind maybe getting us some coffee while we wait?'"

"I said, 'Why, sure, how do y'all take your coffee?' And I got coffee for each of them.

"Then they said, 'We really are on a tight schedule, so if you wouldn't mind getting Mr. Cameron.'

"And I said, 'Well, that would be impossible.' They asked why, and I said, 'Well, because Mr. Cameron died fifteen years ago.'

"And they said, 'What do you mean he died fifteen years ago?'

"And then I said, 'Well, it's not really that hard to understand. He had a heart attack and died.'

"'Well, then, who took over his law practice?' this joker wanted to know.

"I said, 'Took it over, nobody took it over. His partner, J. Cameron just continued the practice,' I said with a wink. Well, honey, finally, in came the dawn. I'd never seen so many suits look so befuddled. I told them to enjoy their coffee and that my time was as precious as theirs and that my clock began the very moment they asked me to get them coffee. I know I don't look like the usual lawyer, so I like to have a little fun with it."

I began to laugh, and then I honestly couldn't stop. "Oh, dear Lord," I said, gasping for air, "that's the funniest thing I've ever heard."

"Well, stick around, darling, I got more where that came from. Well, now, I've gone and taken up enough of your time. C'mon. Jimmy's back this way, and he's expecting you."

"Jimmy, your appointment's here!" Judy bellowed.

I followed her into an office at the back of the building. James Carmichael, or Jimmy, as she called him, wasn't exactly what I expected either.

"Jimmy, this here's Ellen Williams. Ellen Williams, may I present my partner, Jimmy Carmichael," Judy said.

"It's nice to meet you, Ellen," he said, wiping his hands on a greasy napkin and making his way around the desk to shake my hand.

Jimmy's abundant graying hair was badly in need of a trim, along with his thick eyebrows. A ruddy complexion, a rather large nose, and an electric smile completed his kind face. If I were to guess, I'd say he was in his early sixties. He carried a few extra pounds around the middle, straining the buttons on his stained white shirt. His sleeves were rolled up and his tie hung loosely from his collar. I caught him finishing up what was left of his meatball hoagie.

"Please, please, have a seat. Thanks, Judy. I guess Sheila's out for the rest of the day?"

Yep, her sitter called and said the baby was running a fever. Teething, she thinks. Looks like she won't be back in today. That's okay. The voicemail can pick up the calls, and the afternoon looks pretty light. It was real nice meeting you, Ellen."

"Very nice meeting you, too," I said. And I meant it.

As soon as Judy left, Jimmy said, "So, it's nice to finally meet you."

"Thank you, it's nice to meet you too. But I have to tell you, I'm totally at a loss as to why Mrs. Caldwell named me as the owner of her incredible property. I know my lawyer, Greg Blackburn, filled you in on my total shock over this inheritance. I didn't know her or the judge. It makes no sense. I came here hoping you might be able to shed some light on this for me."

"Well, like I told your lawyer on the phone, Mrs. Caldwell really didn't go into detail as to why she made the decision she did. She came in a few years ago and said she wanted to make changes to her will. I remember she was very adamant about the house, wanting to make sure it went to this designated person, which, of course, turned out to be you. Early last year, after she'd been diagnosed with pancreatic cancer, she came in with a photograph of you. She asked that I be sure, in the event of her death, to hold onto the photo as proof she meant for you to have the property."

"You mean there was no further explanation from

her?" I asked.

"It's been awhile, but let me think," he rubbed his chin in contemplation. "Wait a minute. I do remember her saying something about bequeathing her most prized possession would be her act of contrition. Because it meant the most to her, it was the most valuable, like giving a piece of her heart, or something to that effect. She quoted a Bible verse, I think from Isaiah, but I couldn't tell you now which it was."

"Wait, in her Bible, yes… I'll admit, I was doing a little detective work at her house," I said with an embarrassed grin. "I found a marked passage from Isaiah. I didn't know what it meant. Act of contrition? What on earth would she mean by that?" I was totally perplexed.,

"Yep, quite sure that's what she said. I can't imagine what she'd have to feel guilty about. She was a sweet and godly lady. I can tell you this, she knew what she wanted and was firm about her intentions. She was always direct. She might have been small in stature, but underneath, you knew she was one strong lady. I really don't know much more than that. She had many friends from the Brunswick Women's Club. But, to tell you the truth, I think she outlived most of them. Anyway, you might check with them, or her church. I think it was the Episcopal Church here in town. They might give you some leads of some folks who knew her and maybe could shed some light on your situation. Asides from that, I don't have much more I can tell you."

"Well, thank you. I really appreciate your time. If you think of anything else, can I leave my number? Please, call me if you remember anything more," I said as I scribbled my name and number on a Post-it note I retrieved from my purse.

"I sure will. Oh, of course," he said slapping the palm of his hand to his forehead, "I don't know why I forgot this, but her nephew. She had a nephew, a surgeon who lives here. Can't believe I forgot to mention him. Dr. McGaffey, Hunter McGaffey. He is head of cardiology at the hospital. You might speak with him."

"Well, as a matter of fact, I already have. Surprisingly enough, he stopped by this morning out of the blue. We talked. He doesn't know anything either. He's as perplexed as I am," I said.

"Hmm… I guess the old gal had her secrets. We all do, don't we?"

A cold chill went through my body. Those words rendered me speechless for a second.

"You never really know what happens in people's lives," I said, "I won't take up any more of your time. Thank you and it was nice meeting you."

"You are quite welcome. I hope you find what you're looking for. You certainly have inherited one of the more beautiful properties in Brunswick. That property has been in the Caldwell family for years. Truly remarkable," he said. "Oh, here's information regarding the company that manages the property," he said handing me an envelope from the top of his desk. "You can give them a call and they can answer any questions you might have regarding general maintenance of the property and the services they provide."

"Great, thank you. I'll call them. And please, again, if you should think of anything else that might help, Mr. Carmichael, please don't hesitate to call me."

"I promise and please, call me Jimmy"

"Goodbye, Jimmy."

"Goodbye, and good luck."

I left his office feeling like I had gained a bit more insight into Mrs. Caldwell, and yet it was obvious that I'd have to do a lot more investigating.

"Hope you found what you were looking for!" Judy called out, just as I was leaving.

I turned around, and she was standing outside her office door. I imagined not much gets past Judy Cameron.

"No, not really, but Jimmy was able to give me a little more information."

My disappointment, I'm sure, was written on my face. I was really hoping for more.

"Oh, honey, don't fret. This might be a fairly big city, but it's really just a small town. Ask around. You might find more of what you're looking for. She was well known around here. Someone's bound to know somethin'."

"Maybe. I hope so."

"Hey, you want to maybe get something cold to drink? I'm literally done for the day, and you look like you could use a drink."

"That sounds absolutely wonderful," I said.

"Okay, hon, let me grab my pocketbook and let Jimmy know I'm gone. I know just the place. I'm parked out back, but I'll swing around the front and you can follow me over. Meet you out front in a sec."

And, just like that, I had a new friend and was sitting in a nearby café right on the water. It was too hot to sit outside, but the view of the of the marina from the restaurant was pretty.

We each ordered a glass of white wine and enjoyed the lazy afternoon. Somehow, it felt like I had known this woman forever, and yet, I didn't know she existed an hour and a half ago.

"So, tell me about yourself," Judy said.

"Not all that much to tell. I'm from Louisville. I'm married to a guy who happens to be dealing with the possibility of prostate cancer right now. He's a trooper. We'll get through it. I have two adult children, one girl, one boy. Mia lives in Boston with her boyfriend. She's working in public relations and he's in sales. Alex lives in Louisville and has a four-year-old daughter, Rebecca. I adore her. Let's see, I own a small retail business called Ellen's—real original, isn't it—that hopefully is managing without me for a while. We sell unique home decor, jewelry, and clothing made by Kentucky artists. We do all right. I wanted something different after I got out of education and wasn't ready to retire. So, what started out as a kind of a hobby turned into a new occupation. I've got a terrific manager though, so it frees me up a bit. Lately, however, I've been thinking about possibly letting the business go."

"Why's that?"

"Dan's health, business monotony, desire to travel, more time to discover the meaning of life," I said with a smile and a wink. "To tell you the truth, I don't really know what I want. That's one of the reasons I decided to come. I'm hoping it will give me some time to reflect, while at the same time giving me something new and exciting to think about. Let's see, I brought my three-year-old golden retriever named Lilly with me for companionship, and, for the life of me, I don't know why I'm here. That's about it. What about you?"

"Well, I've been practicing law for what seems like forever. I was one of only two women in law school. I was blond, the other was brunette. I got the most handsome lawyer of the bunch. Don't tell me blondes don't have more fun!" she laughed. "My husband and I opened up the practice over twenty-five years ago. We were doing pretty good as a husband-and-wife duo until he up and had a massive heart attack in court. Goin' on fifteen years now."

"Oh, Judy, I'm so sorry."

"Well, don't be. We had a hell of a good run. He was

a good man. Louder than me, if you can believe it. But a good man. He left me with a son to raise and a business to run. I brought Jimmy in almost immediately after Joe died. We just clicked, and I trusted him. My mama always told me to follow my instincts, and I did. Jimmy's solid. No finer man or partner. I've been blessed."

"That's good to hear. You seem pretty happy."

"Oh, darlin', I am, I truly am. And you should be pretty happy, too, especially if you decide to sell that property. You're sitting on a gold mine!"

"Oh, heavens, I haven't even thought about it. I'm just trying to figure out why she left it to me."

"You know, I've seen a lot of crazy things in my career. People doing things out of spite, people doing things out of hate, people doing things out of love. I didn't know Mrs. Caldwell well, but I can tell you this, if she wanted you to have that property, she had a real good reason for it. You just gotta find the connection to her," she said.

"Well, how do I do that? I don't know where to begin."

"Ha, honey, you already have. You've already got more information today than you had yesterday, correct?"

"Yes, that's true."

"Well, then, that's something," she said, taking a long gulp of wine. Condensation from the humid day gathered on the glass.

"How would you go about it if you were me?"

"That house probably holds the key. There is something in that house that will lead you to the answer. Or maybe clues to where to look next. I would also bet that the real key lies up here," she stated, tapping her head.

"You mean, you have the answer?" I laughed.

She smiled, "*You* have the answer. You just don't know it yet. There's an obvious connection. Whether it's directly connected to you, or maybe someone you know, but mark my word, there's a connection. And you, missy, hold the key."

I took a sip of my wine and contemplated what she said.

"Well, if I do, it's certainly hiding from me. Judy. I know we just met, but do you think maybe I could call on you in the future if I need some help? I could really use a friend in town."

"Darlin, you can call on me anytime," she said as she grabbed a pen from her purse and wrote down her cell number.

"Here, let me give you mine too. In case you maybe find anything you think might be beneficial, or if you'd just like to grab another glass of wine," I said holding up the almost empty glass. "In fact, you ought to come out and see the property. Maybe bring your tennis shoes, and we can wander a bit."

"I'd love to. I haven't been out to the Caldwells' place for eons. Let me think. The last time I remember being there was for a fundraiser they hosted for one of their many charities. Gorgeous place."

"Then you must come. I don't know how long I'll be here, but I'll call you."

We finished our wine and promised to get together soon. I had a feeling Judy and I would remain friends. She appeared to be such a strong and confident lady. A lawyer with her own practice, a widow, and a single mother. She's faced some adversity. Jenny had that kind of spirit at one time. I was always more of the introvert, Jenny the extrovert. She wasn't afraid of much of anything. When I think of her now, the guilt seeps through. Could I have done something more to save her that day?

2016

Ten

It was late afternoon when Sharon and I got back to the hotel. We'd spent the better part of the day enjoying a mostly liquid lunch, and we were ready to stretch out on our beds, maybe watch some TV, or take a cat nap. We were hot and sticky and relieved to be in air conditioning. No sooner had we reached our room when my phone rang. It was my mother.

"Hi, Mom. What'd you find out? Anything?" I asked throwing my purse on the hotel bed and kicking off my sandals, wiping the sweat that was trickling down the back of my neck.

"Ellen, Ellen, I, I can't believe," she stammered. "I can't believe it, she's, she's gone."

My heart stopped. "What do you mean she's gone?"

"Oh God...!!" came the wail of my mother. "Oh my God, I failed her, I failed her!"

"Mom, oh God, Mom, what happened, what's going on?" I spluttered.

"They couldn't revive her; they couldn't get her to wake up. Pills, she took some pills, Oh, God, I couldn't help her."

"Mom, I'm so, so sorry. I'm coming home, Mom. I'm coming home."

I can't remember much of the flight home. I was too numb. Though my sister had been out of my life for some time, she was still my sister. I thought about all the wasted time. I thought about how close we had once been, and then how far apart. I remember it began to get even worse as she entered adulthood. Depression, maybe. We always called it the blues, but for Jenny, the blues never seemed to go away. Even now we couldn't quite understand it. Jenny wouldn't let any of us into her world. She would keep you at arm's length. She had shown signs at an even earlier age of being combative, angry, and sometimes cold. So much time had passed, and Jenny seemed incapable of maintaining relationships with anybody but her husband. She'd breeze into your life showing up out of the blue or randomly phone here and there. Just as quickly, she'd breeze out. It wasn't as much of a breeze as it was a windstorm. Jenny never left quietly. She stormed out, announcing her resentment, and was always the victim. I hated her. I loved her. I was so angry with her.

From the information that was gathered, and according to Mike, Jenny had been acting strange all day. Well, I guess, stranger than normal. She was extremely quiet and despondent. She told Mike she just wasn't feeling well. Mike believed her. She thought a nice soak in the tub would help. It was only when Jenny had been in the bathroom for over an hour, supposedly soaking in the tub, that Mike knew something was wrong. He tried to open the door, but it was locked and there was no response when he called her name. She had taken an entire bottle of pills, later determined to be barbiturates, and washed them down with a pint of vodka. She then placed a hand towel behind her head in the tub, lit a candle, laid her cell phone on the tub's edge, and went to permanent sleep. Mike managed to get the door open, but it was too late. When EMS arrived, no amount of CPR was going to revive her. And her last phone call, well, that was to me.

Her funeral reflected Jenny's odd personality. Just a handful of mourners. The sad thing was that I wouldn't say that those in attendance were truly mourners, just people who felt obligated in some way to show up. She had no children to mourn her. My brothers were present, out of obligation to our Mom. They didn't have much to say, having been estranged from Jenny for years. They simply had no relationship with her. My kids came out of respect for their grandmother and me. Mia and Alex had relatively few memories of their aunt. Those they did have were mostly of family gatherings when Jenny would make a rare appearance. I was just glad they came. I not only appreciated their support, but they helped fill some of the empty space in our hearts and in the room. A few small flower arrangements and a peace lily delivered to the funeral home flanked the closed casket. One arrangement in particular caught my eye. It was a solitary rose in a white-beaded vase adorned with a pink ribbon. The card read: "Let the little children come to me and do not hinder them, for to such belongs the kingdom of heaven. Matthew 19:14." There was no signature. Jenny did have a few odd acquaintances. In life, she spent a great deal of time with a small group of women from her church. On the rare occasions when Jenny would drift back into my life, she would always talk in affirmations and quotes. "My life is my message," written by Mahatma Gandhi, or "Better to be a lion for a day, than a sheep all your life," by Elizabeth Kenny. It was like she was constantly trying to fool herself into having a reason to go on. Instead of just living, her life appeared lifelike. I guess it was her way of validating her life, showing that it mattered. I didn't know. All I knew was that she was gone.

 She was buried next to a lovely maple tree on a hill in a small cemetery outside Louisville. The ceremony concluded at the gravesite with a few words from an elderly lady. I suspected she was a member of her church group, but I didn't think it mattered enough now to even ask Mike how this lady was connected to Jenny. Her name was Mildred and she was a rather large, gray-haired, matronly looking woman in her mid-seventies. Mildred was wearing a shapeless purple and green paisley dress, more like a sack. Her swollen legs were encased in support hose and her feet were stuffed into black orthopedic shoes. She looked like she ached with every step. She laboriously got up from her white folding chair and stood in front of the grave. I was really hoping that Mildred's words might give us all some insight into the real Jenny. But it soon became apparent that I wouldn't be getting any more information regarding Jenny's state of mind or answers to my sister's long-held mysteries. Mildred simply said she would miss their afternoons on the phone or the occasional game of Scrabble. I know this sounds awful, but I almost laughed. *That's it, that's the eulogy, phone calls and Scrabble? Please, dear God, let there be a bit more said about my life than that*, I thought. Then the guilt settled in. How could I judge what Jenny's life had become, what she valued? Maybe she was just as content with phone conversations and Scrabble as I was with the things that gave me pleasure. I didn't really believe that though. As a kid she had been a force to reckon with, a mini-tornado. Phone conversations and Scrabble with an elderly woman just didn't match that force of nature I knew as a young girl. *When did it all go so terribly wrong for you, Jenny?* I let out a sigh and turned to the rest of the family. My brothers, Jack and Kendall, were assisting Mom as she said her last goodbyes to my sister. There were a few hugs for Mike, a few hugs shared by my brothers and I, and a hug from each of us for our mom. Kendall agreed to take Mom home. I stood next to Dan watching everyone descend to their cars.

"Can I have a moment?" I asked Dan.

"Absolutely, take all the time you need," he said. "We'll wait for you in the car." I gave them each a hug, and I told them I loved them. I was so thankful to have my family with me.

I stared at the freshly disturbed earth, and then I said to Jenny, "I'm so sorry I couldn't help you. I hope you're at peace, lady. God knows you spent your life trying to find it. Maybe it was never here in the physical world for you in the first place. Maybe you had to find your peace elsewhere. You know I've always loved you; I just think most of us didn't know how to reach you." I stood there for several minutes, and I smiled as an image of the two of us came to mind. I asked her, "Do you remember the day the mouse got loose in our room and we screamed and shimmied up the wardrobe? We sat there, scrunched together on the top of that old wardrobe, holding hands and screaming for Mom. She came running in with baby Kendall on one hip and a full laundry basket on the other. She had been out back hanging clothes on the line. At the same time, we both started yelling that there was a mouse loose in the bedroom. Mom laughed, then we started laughing. We never did find that damn mouse. Do you remember, do you remember how we all laughed that day?" I said, bending my head to let the tears come, but they wouldn't come. "There was a time once when we had fun together, when we were close. When we weren't thinking about sickness or anger, or other scary things. I hope you find the kind of life you always wanted on the other side. I hope you find love and happiness, and, above all, I hope you find peace. Goodbye, Jenny. You may not believe this, but I love you."

As I began to make my way back to the car, I heard what sounded like a faint bird—*caw*! I kept walking. Then, there it was again. I finally stopped and slowly looked back over my shoulder. Sitting on a low branch of that maple tree was a large black bird, maybe a crow, I couldn't really tell from where I stood. I was too far away to see exactly what kind of bird it was. But, as I stood there watching it, as if in a trance, I could almost swear I heard it say, "Ello Enry!" before it lifted its wings and flew away. I shivered.

Eleven

It was well past the dinner hour by the time I made my way back to the house. I'll bet Lilly was starving, although, judging by her robust frame, I think she could afford to miss a meal or two. She must have heard the car pull up because as I ascended the front porch steps, I could see her canine snout pressed up against the side panel of the front door, eagerly awaiting my arrival.

"Hi girl, did you miss me?" I said, entering the foyer, and giving her a good scratch behind her ears. "C'mon, I think there might be a can of food with your name on it. Let's go eat."

After feeding Lilly and fixing myself an omelet and toast, I picked up my meager plate, a chilled glass of Pinot Grigio, and my laptop and made my way to the couch. It was time to do some research.

"Okay, let's see if we can begin to find some answers," I said to no one. *What do I already know? I know where Madeline and the judge met, well, sort of. I know she had friends from both her church and her women's club. Aha! Okay, those are two places where I can begin.*

I spent the next hour googling the judge and Madeline. I realized I was slipping into referring to Mrs. Caldwell as Madeline. Maybe I was feeling a personal connection with this lady, though I didn't know her at all. There were several articles on the judge and his landmark decisions while on the bench. There were blurbs in the local paper about the charities they were involved in and the impact each made on their community. The judge served on several boards around town. Madeline participated in charities that mainly involved children, such as the national organizations of Make a Wish, St. Jude, and The March of Dimes. She was also heavily involved with the local children's hospital, and the promotion of the arts for youth in the Brunswick community. There were countless accolades for her role in the work she did with children through her church. I made a list of possible contacts, phone numbers, and addresses. I wondered whether it would be best to drop in on some of those places instead of calling first. In the end I decided I'd reach out by phone to some of these folks, to see if I could take just a few minutes of their time. I took another sip of wine, contemplating my next move, when the phone rang.

"Hi, sweetie, how was your day?

"Well, hello! My day was crazy busy. What about yours? Any progress on your mystery fairy godmother?" asked Dan.

"Not a lot as of yet. How are you?"

"I'm good. I spent most of the day putting out fires, but other than that, glad to be home."

"Did you get anything to eat?"

"Yeah, I stopped off at Impellizzeri's and got a pizza."

"Oh, I am so jealous! My omelet can't compete with a slice of heaven," I laughed.

"You're right about that," he chuckled. "So, what happened at the lawyer's office?"

I quickly brought him up to speed and told him about my delightful new friend Judy Cameron, as well as my encounter with Hunter McGaffey. The concern in Dan's voice was apparent. "Ellen, you need to be careful. You really don't know what or who you're dealing with there. You may meet some really pissed off folks over this, this… I don't even know what to call it. This situation, I guess."

"I know, and I hear what you're saying, but I really don't think I'm in any harm. Dr. McGaffey was gracious enough. I didn't feel threatened. I honestly think he's as baffled by his aunt's actions as we are," I said.

"Well, you know if you want me to come, just say the

word, and I'll make my way down there."

"You just miss Lilly, admit it," I laughed.

He chuckled, "You bet I do! I really miss her waking me up at 5:00 a.m. to take her out to do her business."

"Now I know you're lying," I joked. "She's been a good girl, exploring the house, chasing squirrels, barking at the ducks. I think she's going to miss this place when we're back home."

"I think *you're* going to miss that place when you're back," he said.

"I probably will. It such a special property. Madeline must have loved it so much. Just wish I knew what her motives were for leaving it to me. I've made some headway. I just spent time on the Internet trying to come up with some new leads about her life. Tomorrow I'm going to make some calls and see if I can meet with some of the folks that knew her best."

"Where will you start?"

"Most likely her church. I'm hoping I can speak with the minister. He might be able to give me some names of parishioners she became friends with. I've been told that she rarely missed a Sunday service, so I figure that's the best place to start," I said. "I'm going to try and reach him this evening."

"Watch out for those church folks, they can be cunning. They'll have you donating the entire property *in the name of Jesus,"* he said sounding like an overly enthusiastic television evangelist.

"Maybe that's not such a bad idea," I said jokingly.

"Really!"

"Nah, if Mrs. Caldwell's act of contrition involved the church, she would've left her estate to them, I'm sure. This old gal had something else in mind. I just don't know. But I'll keep turning over rocks and see what I can find."

"Well, you know what you sometimes find when you turn over rocks?"

"A giant centipede?" I chided.

"Exactly."

"Ellen, you know I love you?"

"I know, I love you too. And I know you're struggling right now. I'm not really sure why I feel the need to go it alone on this one. I've always needed you with me. I feel guilty for not being with you now while you're dealing with this damn prostate thing. You and the kids must think I'm awful and insensitive to your needs."

"First of all, you have always stood by my side since the day I married you. It works both ways, and I know if you feel this strongly about what you're doing, I'm supporting you in this, and, as far as the kids, since when did we start listening to them?" he laughed.

I smiled. Though we've had our share of problems, I

did love this man.

"Well, I will be home when it's time for you to see the doctor, regardless of what's going on here. And, if you need me before then, just let me know."

"I will, but there's nothing either of us can do right now. Sitting around playing Grim Reaper as we wait for test results won't help either of us. You take care of business, and I'll be here when you get back."

"I don't deserve you," I said honestly.

"Aw, shucks!" He said in his best Goofy voice. "With those kind words you're going to make me blush," he joked.

"No, really. I mean it."

"I feel that same way, Ellen. Everything's going to be okay. Now, go play detective and solve this thing!" he ordered.

"Okay, sweetie! I'll keep you posted on any progress. Take care! I love you!"

"Love you too, bye."

"Bye," I said, but he'd already hung up.

I was too tired to stare at the computer anymore, so I quickly closed the laptop and took my dish to the sink. I poured myself a second glass of wine and spent the next hour wandering the house, looking for some clues possibly tucked away somewhere. Maybe there was a note in a drawer, a card she had received, or a journal of some kind. I knew that at her request, no one was to be given access to the house except for me, her lawyer, and the property managing service, at least that's what Jimmy had told me. So, if that was true, no one had been there to remove anything, just to clean and fill the vases with fresh-cut flowers from the estate grounds. I wandered around downstairs for a bit, looking in drawers and side tables in the living room, but I didn't find anything of value. Tall built-in bookcases showcased lovely silver-framed photographs of children's happy faces—a family gathering on Christmases and summer picnics. There was a black-and-white photograph taken of what looked like a young and handsome Hunter McGaffey, in his teenage years standing next to his uncle. It was shocking how much Hunter looked like the judge. It was a beautiful family, happy and having a good time. I still wasn't finding anything that would help me, so I thought maybe Madeline's bedroom might be the more logical place to look. I began making my way upstairs when I realized something. I turned around and went back downstairs to make sure I was correct in my thinking. It wasn't what was there that was so telling, it's what wasn't there. Out of all those photographs, I hadn't seen a single picture of a younger Madeline Caldwell in any of the frames. Not even a wedding photo could be found. In fact, her picture hadn't even appeared in the Internet searches. The only picture I had seen so far was the beautiful older lady that sat next to her bed, and I had just assumed that was her.

I went to her bedroom and picked up the photograph of this elderly lady, still feeling that she somehow looked familiar. I felt guilty, but I took the picture out of its frame and looked on the back for a name or date. Nothing. "Okay, I'm taking you with me for just a short period of time, Madeline, if this is you. I promise to put you back, but for now, you're coming with me." I suddenly felt very tired. I hadn't chosen a room to sleep in and I didn't feel like dragging bags up the steps. I slept well on the den couch, and even though there were plenty of bedrooms to choose from, I still felt odd making myself at home. So, for now, it was going to be the couch. I would leave all of this for tomorrow. *Come on, Madeline, let's go to bed.*

I changed into my pajamas, brushed my teeth, and washed my face in the downstairs powder room. I made a last check of all the locks and made sure the alarm was set. I grabbed a book I had been trying to finish for the past few weeks, plopped down on the couch with Lilly, and settled in for the night. I tried to concentrate, but I found myself reading a paragraph and realizing I didn't even know what I'd read. I finally gave up and put the book down. I picked up the photograph of my mystery lady from the coffee table where I'd placed it when I came downstairs.

I held it in front of me. "Who are you?"

I stared at it for a few seconds, and for some reason I could hear Jenny's voice in my head.

"Hey, Ellen. Today's picture day at school. What are you gonna wear?"

Twelve

Jenny was in fifth grade, and I was in fourth. I was wearing my crisp white blouse with the Peter Pan collar, a double-breasted red vest with brass buttons, a dark plaid skirt, bobby socks, and saddle oxfords. My ash-blond hair hung just above my shoulders and my long bangs were pulled back and fastened with a gold barrette. The real star of my ensemble, though, was a pair of pink cat-eye glasses that adorned my heart-shaped face. Jenny had on a white blouse buttoned all the way up to the neck, a dark green sweater, a blue and gray pleated skirt, bobby socks, and penny loafers. She wore her long blond hair with straight bangs and a plastic red headband that finished the look. Picture day was special. It always came in the fall, and you knew you'd better look your best because you were going to see that godforsaken picture on the living room bookshelf for the rest of your natural-born life. It was bad enough I had to look at my pictures from kindergarten through third grade every time I ran out the front door. These images were imprinted on my brain.

"Don't forget your lunches, girls!" hollered Mom. "Oh, and girls, you've got to go over to Mrs. Cooper's after school today. I've got to drive Aunt June and Charlie to Charlie's afternoon doctor's appointment. I'll have to pick up Jack from his school first, so he's coming with us. I don't know how long I'll be, but Mr. and Mrs. Cooper are expecting you right after school, so don't dawdle."

"Aww, Mom, no! We can stay by ourselves, we're not babies," Jenny protested.

"Don't argue with me. You won't be over there that long," she said flatly.

I really didn't mind going over to the Coopers. They were a nice enough couple that lived two houses down from us in the cul-de-sac, next door to Miss Gallagher's. Mrs. Cooper was a rather plump lady who wore her dark hair piled high on her head and twisted in a French roll. Mr. Cooper was a tall, thin, guy who wore his hair in a crew cut and greeted you with a nod most of the time. He rarely spoke, but, boy, could he play the organ. Well, he and Mrs. Cooper both played, and they had a giant organ that dominated an entire wall of their tiny living room. They were faithful church goers, and Mrs. Cooper was the organist for her church. On warm days, when folks left their windows open, you could hear the discordant, bellowing notes coming from their house.

I was always fascinated with the organ pipes, and a little scared of them too. Maybe because organ music always seemed to accompany a scary movie. Anyway, the Coopers would let us play theirs.

"We can play the organ," I said a little too enthusiastically for Jenny's liking as I stuck my nose in my brown paper sack to see what Mom made for lunch.

"Who cares? I don't want to go."

"You're going! Now, get moving. I'm not going to stand here and argue with you anymore. We have enough problems with Charlie and your brother both being sick. Hurry up, or you'll be late for school," Mom ordered as she gave Jenny her "don't challenge me" stare.

And, with that, we went to school.

After school, Jenny was waiting for me out front near the flagpole. I spotted her immediately as I descended the school steps. Jenny was a bit taller than everyone else. I couldn't quite put it into words, but even if there were a sea of people, she always kind of stood out. I raced down the steps, elated to be done with school.

"Did you get your picture taken? Our class did. The teachers passed out little combs for us to fix our hair. Billy Sanders thumped his comb against Molly Crandell's cheek, and she screamed so loud it almost busted my eardrum," I said laughing. "She had a big red mark across her face before her picture was taken. I'll bet that's a picture she'll never forget."

"I would've socked him. He'd look great with two black eyes for his picture," Jenny said with authority.

I could see my older sister doing just that, turning around and flattening him to the floor. I smiled just thinking about it. Billy was a bully and Jenny hated bullies. Of course, she was a bit of one herself.

"Let's stop at the Quart and Loaf and get some candy before we go home," Jenny said rather mischievously.

"Mom said to come straight home. We gotta go to the Coopers."

"So? It won't take five minutes to run in there and get some candy. C'mon, I got some change, and we can get a sack of penny candy."

The Quart and Loaf was the little market that was practically in our backyard. The only thing that separated this small mom-and-pop grocery store from our house was the alley in the back and a row of twelve-foot hedges that spanned the length of our yard. We had a small opening where the hedges began, and that's where we'd cut through. We passed through that opening so many times, we had trampled a path.

"Okay, let's go," I said. "Race ya!" I bolted across the school parking lot, clutching my books.

We reached the store in less than three minutes and had to stop outside to catch our breath.

"Hey, isn't that Mr. Jameson's car?" I said between gulps of air.

"Yeah, it's looks like it," Jenny replied, equally winded.

Parked in front of the store was the distinct red-and-white Ford Fairlane that the younger Mr. Jameson drove. I remembered his name was Henry, because that's what that bird would call out. *Ello Enry.* Alone in the passenger seat was his wife, the lady we referred to as Crazy Mae.

"Isn't that his wife?" I asked.

"Yeah, that's her," Jenny said.

"She's staring at us."

"Don't stare back. C'mon, let's go in," Jenny said.

Still breathing a little heavily, I followed her into the store, but I could feel that lady's eyes on me as I turned my back. It felt spooky, and, if that wasn't enough, this store made me feel a little depressed. It always seemed a bit gloomy. No matter the time of day, or even the season, the store took on that feeling of cloudiness. I never understood why. Maybe it was because of the colorless walls or the dismal speckled-gray linoleum floor. I was looking down at the floors when a long shadow crossed our path.

"Well, hello, lassies. What are you gals up to?" said a very tall gentleman who was blocking our way to the candy aisle.

It was Henry, the old man's son, Crazy Mae's husband. He was much taller than his father and had a mop of really thick, sandy hair. He had a handsome face, but his complexion was a bit weathered, like someone who had spent a long time out in the sun. He was carrying a small grocery sack in one hand and a pack of Lucky Strike cigarettes in the other. He smiled widely, showing a row of tobacco-stained teeth.

"Just getting some candy, and we're in a hurry," Jenny stated as she grabbed my hand.

"Important business you have to tend to?" he asked with a grin.

I didn't know what to say to him, so I said, "How's Bird?"

"Why, Bird's fine. You come over and visit him sometime. He'd love to see you. You girls can come over anytime you'd like, an-y-time," he said, enunciating the word as he looked directly at Jenny.

"Well, uh, maybe sometime. Our mom's not home and we gotta go over to the Coopers' today."

"Shut up!" Jenny whispered as she turned her back to him and looked at me.

"Yeah, maybe some time, bye," I replied timidly.

I never heard if he responded because Jenny grabbed my arm and practically dragged me down the next aisle. "Hey, this isn't the candy aisle," I protested, as loaves of Sunbeam, jars of Jif, and paper products whizzed past my head. Jenny stopped at the end of the aisle without putting on the brakes, and I practically fell on top of her. She put her finger to her lips as a signal for me to shut the hell up. I did. She waited a moment until she was sure Henry Jameson was gone.

"What's wrong with you?" I shouted.

"I don't like him! He gives me the creeps!" she said.

I just shrugged my shoulders, rolled my eyes, and went around her to look for the Bazooka bubble gum.

After making our candy purchases, we cut through the hedges and made our way to the Coopers', circling our own house and yard to get there. Our pockets were filled with every dentist's dream for continued business: bubble gum, Tootsie Rolls, and jawbreakers. We were almost at the Coopers' door when we heard the crunch of tires on the gravel driveway next door. It was Miss Gallagher coming home. She stopped the car at the end of her front sidewalk and got out. She was wearing a long drab green coat with a wide collar and matching gloves. Her carrot-colored cropped hair along with that coat and gloves made her look like one tall olive to me.

"Hello, girls! How are you?" she called over in a nicer greeting than we had heard from her in the past. "Are you visiting the Coopers today?"

"We're fine, Miss Gallagher. We're going to stay here until our mom comes home," I answered.

"Oh! Everything alright?" she asked.

"Yeah, our baby cousin's sick and our mom drove our aunt to the doctor's office. So, we gotta stay with the Coopers until she comes home," I volunteered.

"Oh! I see," she said as she thumbed through the letters she had retrieved from her mailbox. "Well, you girls have fun with the Coopers."

"Okay, bye."

"Bye-bye," she said while waving her hand as if to dismiss us as she unlocked her door.

"Bitch," Jenny muttered.

"Jenny, she was actually nice for once," I said, defending her.

"She's still a bitch," Jenny snarled.

Mrs. Cooper greeted us with a warm welcome and told us to come in and make ourselves at home. She had made us brownies and fresh-squeezed lemonade. What a sugar-filled afternoon we would have.

"Mr. Cooper's not home from work yet, and I'm trying to make his favorite cake. It's his birthday, and I had promised him red velvet," she said, looking almost giddy with the excitement of fulfilling her husband's ultimate birthday wish.

"That's real nice, Mrs. Cooper," was all I could think to say.

"Well, here, you girls just make yourselves at home," and she gestured to the area in front of the television.

I was perfectly content sitting on the rug, in front of their brand new black-and-white Silvertone television, eating brownies, drinking ice-cold lemonade, and finishing it off with a jawbreaker the size of a golf ball. Jenny, on the other hand, wasn't content to watch TV. As soon as she polished off her snack, she hopped up and announced she wanted to go home to change her clothes and get a couple of board games. She didn't like sitting on the floor wearing her skirt. She went to the kitchen doorway and told Mrs. Cooper what she was going to do. Jenny never even considered asking permission.

"I promise I'll just run over to the house really quick, and I'll be right back."

"Well, I suppose that would be alright," said Mrs. Cooper rather hesitantly.

"I'll go with you," I said.

Mrs. Cooper stood in the doorway. "No, Ellen, let your sister go. I don't want both of you out and about."

"Jenny, be quick," said Mrs. Cooper.

"I'll be right back, I swear," Jenny promised.

"Hey, bring my Barbie case, would ya?" I asked. Barbies were my favorite thing in the whole world.

"Maybe," she called back as she slammed the front door.

"That girl is a ball of energy, isn't she," Mrs. Cooper quipped, shaking her head as she walked back into the kitchen.

I was totally engrossed in after-school cartoons when Mr. Cooper came walking through the front door.

"Well, hello there. What a nice surprise," Mr. Cooper said while looking around for his wife.

"Hi, Mr. Cooper. Mrs. Cooper's in the kitchen. Happy Birthday!" I exclaimed.

"Well, thank you! How did you know?"

Mrs. Cooper must have heard the conversation and came in wiping her hands on her bright yellow apron.

"Hi dear," and then she instantly turned to me and asked, "Where's your sister?"

"I dunno," I shrugged.

She glanced at her watch and said, "Dear Lord, it's been over an hour. I've been so busy in the kitchen, I forgot all about her."

"I'll go find her," I said.

"No, wait, we'll go find her together. I don't want anyone else getting lost. Give me a minute while I wash my hands. Jim, the cake just came out of the oven, so don't you dare go sampling anything before I can frost it. We'll be back in a minute, once we find her sister."

It was after six o'clock when Mrs. Cooper and I made our way over to the house. It was beginning to get dark earlier now, showing signs of the changing of the seasons. The air was cooler. We were lucky that it had stayed warmer last week when we were out trick-ortreating and were able to wear our costumes without our coats covering them up. We both called out Jenny's name as we made our way to our house. Jenny wasn't anywhere outside that we could see. We hurried up our driveway, scraping through the gravel. We passed through the carport that served as our poor man's garage and headed to the back of the house. Mom always left the back door unlocked, never worrying about a thing. She said it was easier to keep it unlocked than to have to hunt for her keys. And besides, she said she'd feel sorry for any thief who robbed this house. Our stuff was so old that they'd have to pay someone to take it off their hands. She said it would be more of a loss for them, and then she laughed.

"Jenny, Jenny! You here?" I yelled as I entered the kitchen and flipped on the overhead light. The stark white walls seemed cold. In fact, the tiny kitchen itself seemed cold with its chipped Formica table. The kitchen chairs with their faded yellow plastic cushions and aluminum legs sat around the table looking rather sad. How many meals had we shared as a family at that table? We entered the living room and called out again. Jenny wasn't there.

"You stay here," commanded Mrs. Cooper. "Let's turn on a light, and I'll go see if she's in any of the back rooms."

"Jenny, dear, are you back there? Jenny? It's Mrs. Cooper, dear. Hello?" Mrs. Cooper continued to call out.

The lights in each bedroom came on as Mrs. Cooper

made her way down the hall, calling out Jenny's name and checking each room. As she flipped on the light in our room something in the air changed. Something was wrong, I knew it. And that's when I heard Mrs. Cooper scream out, "Oh Jenny, dear God, what's happened to you?!"

Thirteen

I awoke to a metallic taste in my mouth and Lilly's wet nose in my hand. Ugh... not the best start to my day. Lilly's head was resting on my leg, patiently waiting for me to stop playing zombie and be a responsible pet owner. I stretched my aching limbs, rubbed my eyes, and sat up on one elbow. Madeline's picture was laying on the floor, so I reached down and set it on the coffee table. Last night, it had triggered some long, forgotten memories of the evening we found Jenny. I hadn't thought about that in an awfully long time.

"Lilly, give me a second, then I'll take you out and feed you," I said as I got up and made my way to the bathroom.

It was another typical summer day in Brunswick. Hot!

As I walked Lilly around the yard, I could already feel the humidity creeping into my core, while beads of sweat dripped between my boobs. A shower would help, but then I'd come right back out into the sweltering Georgia heat. I had a feeling the temperatures were going to reach the nineties. I made a mental note to wear the short-sleeved cotton dress I brought with me since I'd be in town for the better part of the day. I had actually reached Mrs. Caldwell's minister by phone the evening before, the Reverend Gerald Hollister of the Brunswick Episcopal Church. He had agreed to meet with me this morning at 10:00 a.m. in the church office. I didn't go into a lot of detail on the phone, just that I had been the benefactor of a gift from Mrs. Caldwell's estate and that I'd hoped he might be able to answer some questions. He had a pleasant voice, the kind that put you immediately at ease. I could only imagine what he thought of my request to speak with him. Well, honestly, it was all a bit odd, that's for sure.

After a taking a quick shower, gobbling a piece of toast smothered with butter and jam, and washing it down with a cup of strong black coffee, I was ready to head out. I hoped to stop at the Women's Club of Brunswick after the meeting with the reverend. I hadn't been able to reach anyone at the Women's Club by phone, so I thought I'd just pop in and see if I might have any luck. Then maybe stop for lunch somewhere.

I patted Lilly on the head, set the house alarm, and locked the door behind me. I really hoped I would make some progress today. I retrieved my sunglasses from my purse and headed down the steps to the car.

"Okay, Madeline, lead me in the right direction," I said out loud. The only response was from the flock of geese that at that very moment made their entrance onto the pond. I envied those birds, having the ability to fly. It sure beat getting into a stifling hot car.

It was less than a half hour later when I pulled into the church parking lot. I was a few minutes early for my meeting with Reverend Hollister. Like everyone who has a few minutes to spare, I took out my phone to check for messages. With my rushing around this morning, I hadn't even glanced at my phone before taking it off the charger and throwing it in my handbag. Sure enough, I had two voicemails, calls that I must have missed while in the shower. One was from Mia, asking me if all was well and when I might be home. The other was from Dan. He said he didn't want anything in particular, just checking in as he made his way to work. He sounded good, no apparent stress in his voice. A pang of guilt and concern hit me as I thought about his upcoming test results. Was I a terrible person for not being with him right now? If it were the other way around, would I understand his motives for leaving me alone when I was facing possible cancer? I know what he would tell me if he heard my inner voice. He would say I'm being overly dramatic and that I'm wasting energy worrying about something that neither one of us can do anything about. I smiled. I thought about how fortunate I was to have lived with and loved a man for so long that I could literally write his dialogue. Just then, my ringtone sounded, startling me. I almost dropped the phone. The name Hunter McGaffey came across the screen. *Oh boy, what now?* I automatically switched from using the speaker on the car phone to just using my handset. For some reason, the speakerphone made me feel vulnerable. I don't know why. There was no one else to hear my conversation.

"Hello?" I said with as much confidence in my voice I could muster.

"Hello, Ellen. Hunter McGaffey. How are you?"

"I'm fine, and you?" I asked.

"Good, good, thank you. I hope you don't mind me calling. I kind of have a strange request."

"Oh, please, it can't be any stranger than the current situation I've found myself in," I said with a nervous chuckle.

"Well, there's some truth in that," he laughed. "My girls were asking the other day if they might come over and visit their aunt's gravesite and, maybe, if you're available, meet you. That is, if it's convenient? They were quite close to their aunt and she with them. We were wondering if you might have some time this weekend? They never really got to say goodbye. They were at school when she passed away, and their exams kept them from coming home for the funeral. They'd like to pay their respects and place some flowers on her grave."

"Wait, what? Her grave?" I stammered. "You mean she's buried on the property?"

"Yes. She and my uncle are both buried on the east side of the property. It has a really great view. From the site, you can look down and see the Brunswick River and much of the estate. It was one of my aunt's favorite places to go, to think or read or even paint. She dabbled a bit in watercolors," he said. "One of her paintings is hanging in the upstairs hallway."

I was speechless. It had never crossed my mind to ask where she'd been laid to rest. I felt stupid for not having asked someone where she was buried.

"Ellen, are you there?"

"Oh, yes, sorry, I feel a little foolish. I didn't know."

"Well there's nothing to feel foolish about," he said with casual confidence.

I couldn't explain it, but this guy always seemed calm, cool, and collected. I guess being a surgeon, it would behoove both doctor and patient to appear that way.

"Well, of course you and the girls can come over. I'll be there all weekend, so just text me a time that would work for you."

"Great, I'll let you know in the next day or two," he said.

"Okay, I look forward to it."

"Bye for now," he said.

I stared at the phone. Why didn't Jimmy tell me where she was buried? I should have been made aware of that. *Because you never asked, idiot*, said a voice in my head. I sat in the car stewing over my stupidity when I suddenly realized I was late.

"Oh gosh, shit!" I cursed at myself. It was already after ten o'clock, and I was late for my meeting with the reverend.

I quickly got out of the car and entered the side vestibule of the sanctuary as I had been instructed. The air conditioning felt glorious, and the church smelled, well, like a church. What is it that gives almost every church the exact same smell? Maybe the blended aromas of old hymnals, wooden benches, and possibly incense. I don't know, but they seem to share the "common scents" (no pun intended) of spirituality. It's like someone could blindfold you, bring you into an unknown location, and you would know immediately you were in a House of God. I'd hoped I wouldn't burst into flames considering how long it had been since I had entered a church. Surely God would show mercy. Pushing forward I came to the sanctuary. It was a beautiful open space that was much larger and brighter than most churches I had visited. There were tall stained-glass windows, cream-colored walls, and long sleek pews the color of teak wood. The wood used for the pulpit, ministers' chairs, and choir area matched the pews. It was a lovely church. I could almost picture Mrs. Caldwell sitting in one of the pews, wearing her Sunday best, listening intently to the sermon of the week.

I turned right and made my way down a hallway that could only lead to the church offices. I could hear what sounded like people engaged in a conversation, so I followed the voices. In a large office on the right sat a dark-haired gentleman, maybe in his late fifties, glasses perched on the end of his long nose, flipping through what looked to be a stack correspondence of some kind. A woman, maybe in her mid-seventies, with grayish blond hair and wearing silver eyeglasses that were attached by a red cord hanging at the nape of her neck was watering plants on the windowsill. The gentleman, upon seeing me, got up from the desk and extended his hand.

"You must be Mrs. Williams. So pleased to meet you. I'm Gerald Hollister, and this is our church secretary, Mrs. Jackson," he said in a jovial voice.

"Hello, it's nice to meet you both. Thank you so much for meeting me on such short notice," I said.

"Not at all," he said as he gestured for me to take one of the two chairs positioned in front of his desk. Would you like some coffee?"

"Oh, no thanks, I've had some this morning, thank you," I said as I settled in one of the chairs.

"All right then. Mrs. Jackson, would you be so kind as to put these in today's mail?" He handed her a stack of letters. "And, if you wouldn't mind, close the door on your way out."

"Not at all, Reverend. It was nice meeting you, Mrs. Williams. We were all very fond of Mrs. Caldwell," she said as she exited the room.

Did everyone in this town know about my current situation? I thought. It felt so strange.

"Well, now, what can I do for you, Mrs. Williams?" he asked as he folded his hands together and placed them on the desk as if in prayer.

I took a deep breath and began. "Well you see, Reverend, I was notified a few months ago by Mrs. Caldwell's attorney about a sizeable inheritance that had been left to me by Mrs. Caldwell. It turns out that the inheritance was the actual Caldwell house and property surrounding it."

"My goodness, what a gift! There were rumors surrounding the estate, but no one really knew for sure," he said.

"You can imagine how flabbergasted I was when I found out it was all legitimate. You see, I have never met Mrs. Caldwell and never been to this town, and I have no earthly idea why she would leave me this beautiful property. I did some extensive online searches before coming to Brunswick, trying to discover anything I could to make sense of her generous gift. I've even been tempted to hire a private investigator, but, for some reason, I felt the need to do this on my own. I don't know why, and I haven't told anyone but my husband about this. Reverend, I hope we can keep this confidential."

"Of course, Mrs. Williams."

"Please, call me Ellen. Well, I get the feeling that maybe our paths have crossed in some way, and she would want me to keep this whole affair private. I know this must all sound very strange, but I feel in some way I'm supposed to protect her or look out for her or something. Doesn't that sound strange? You must think I'm crazy," I said shaking my head.

"Not at all, Mrs. Caldwell was a private person. She

was highly active in the church and community, and yet very private. She and the judge were faithful parishioners of our church family. They were involved in many of the church events. Mrs. Caldwell sang in our choir. She helped with, well, I couldn't even begin to tell you how many potluck suppers, ice cream socials, and charity drives."

"You say she was a private person. Funny, but from those I've talked to, the common theme appears to be how visible, yet private she was. Do you know she doesn't have any pictures of herself anywhere in the house, with the exception of this one that I found which must have been taken in her later years?" I had slipped her photograph into my purse before I left in hope that someone could verify that it was Madeline. "This is the only photo I could find," I said pulling it out of my bag and handing it to him.

He held it for a moment, then handed it back saying, "Yes, she appears to be a mystery to a lot of folks. You know, come to think of it, I don't believe I've ever seen her picture in any of our church newsletters. That does seem odd, considering the amount of time she's spent participating in church activities. When I get some time, maybe I'll thumb through our church archives and see what I can find. Better yet," he said with a wink, "it might just give Mrs. Jackson something to do besides mail my letters and water my plants."

"That would be great, thank you. I certainly appreciate any help you can give me."

He got up from his desk and said, "Come on, take a

walk with me. I want to show you something."

He led me through the sanctuary and out a set of double doors to an enclosed brick courtyard. It was adorned with lavender blue hydrangeas, yellow daylilies, and ornamental grasses. In the corner of the courtyard was a tall magnolia tree in bloom, and in the center was a Japanese maple tree with a white marble bench underneath it.

"I come out here a lot. If I'm having trouble finding the right words for my sermon or just need a few moments, I'll come out here and enjoy the tranquility."

"I can see why. It's a tranquil little spot. Just made for thinking quiet thoughts, I imagine."

He pointed. "You see that bench? Mrs. Caldwell had it made for the church after the judge died. She only asked that she be allowed to select the verse to be engraved upon it. I assumed it would be a verse dedicated to the judge. But, once I read the inscription, I had a strange feeling that the verse might just be in reference to something or someone else. Maybe it's even about her. I don't think it was ever intended to be a dedication to him."

"Did you ever ask her?"

"No, no I didn't. I guess I felt that if she wanted to share that, she would have. I've learned in my ministry that there is a fine line between guiding members of your flock down a path of spiritual peace versus dragging them down it. You have to be rather delicate at times."

"I guess you might be right. Questioning her might have offended her."

"Quite possibly. There. Go have a look," he said pointing to the bench.

I followed the small pathway to where the bench stood. It was summer in Georgia, but I got goosebumps as I read the words:

> *I live in a high and holy place, but also with the one who is contrite and lowly in spirit, to revive the spirit of the lowly and to revive the heart of the contrite. (Isaiah 57:15)*

Isaiah. There it was again. It must have been significant to her. She had marked it in her Bible, and her attorney had said something to me about a quote from Isaiah. "Her lawyer mentioned something about a conversation he had with her. Something about contrition. What do you think that means, Reverend?"

"I really couldn't say, but it obviously meant something to her, something she felt she or someone she knew needed forgiveness from God for, or hoped to be forgiven for. Who's to say?"

"Is there anything else you can tell me? Anything else you remember that might help?"

"Hmm... Well, now, I do remember this one time when she appeared to let her guard down by accident. It was one afternoon when she volunteered to unpack the children's Bibles. This was, oh goodness, maybe five years ago. The first grade Sunday School class was to receive their first Bibles with their names engraved in gold. We were making sure everyone in the class was receiving one and that their names were spelled correctly. I can still remember her taking out that first Bible and holding it as if it were so fragile it just might break. She held it in her hands and ran her fingers over the front, and then ran her thumb over the name engraved on the bottom right corner of the book. She said something like, 'I remember when I received my first Bible. I was in my Papa's church in Savoy. It was such a special day.'

He continued, "I remember the name Savoy because I'm a jazz enthusiast and Benny Goodman's 'Stompin' at the Savoy' is one of my favorite tunes. 'I thought you were born and raised in Chicago,' I said to her. 'Is Savoy a town close to Chicago?' I just remember her straightening up, like she had just registered her own mistake. She recovered quickly and said, 'It's close enough, and, you know, Reverend, Benny Goodman also wrote "Chicago."' Pretty much diverting the subject. And that was the end of the conversation."

"Savoy, she really said Savoy?" I asked in shock.

"Yes, why? Does that register with you?"

"Yes," I said in disbelief. "Savoy's a small town in Illinois that's home to corn, cows, and soybeans. It's a rural community right outside of Champaign, the town where I was born."

"Really. Well, maybe there's something there," he said.

"Maybe. I suppose there's more than one Savoy in the U.S., but… she really said Savoy? Reverend, my mother and father were married in a little church in Savoy more than sixty years ago. The church where they were married was torn down years ago. I remember my mother mentioning it. But I still have an aunt who lives in Savoy. Oh, my God, Charlie's buried in Savoy."

"Charlie, who's Charlie?"

"He was my baby cousin, Reverend, just an angel," I replied. "He died of leukemia back in the early sixties."

"Oh, I'm sorry to hear that. God calls us up when he's ready for us, not when we're ready," Reverend Hollister said.

"I suppose," I said, not really listening. The screech of a bird brought me back to attention and made me jump.

The Reverend laughed, "Don't be frightened, that's just our resident crow. He comes and goes from time to time."

Perched on a high branch of a magnolia tree sat a large black bird. I placed my hand over my eyes to block the sun so I could see the bird a bit clearer. But I missed it. Just like trying to take a photograph quickly before you lose that perfect shot, the bird spread its wings and flew away. I watched the black speck fly into the distance.

"Reverend Hollister, I can't thank you enough for

your time. I appreciate you meeting with me. If you happen to think of anything else, please call me. You have my number. I'll let myself out."

"You're quite welcome, Ellen. Feel free to join us for Sunday worship while you're in town. We'd love to have you. Good luck finding your answers."

"Thank you, Reverend."

I left the reverend standing in the courtyard. I felt the need to move. My head was spinning, making me feel a bit queasy. I couldn't stand there any longer. I hoped he didn't think I was rude, but I was confused by what I had just learned. It just seemed too much of a coincidence that she would have mentioned Savoy.

I began walking. I passed my car and headed down the street. I just needed to move. I wasn't sure where I was going, but I needed to think. I spotted a Walgreen's drugstore on the corner and decided a cold bottled water would help. Maybe I could find a park bench and just sit and think for a few minutes. I grabbed the water out of the refrigerator section and stood there for a moment, letting the frigid air linger all around me. I could hear my mother's voice, *Shut that door! You're letting all the cold air out.* I smiled. *Yes, I am, Mom, and what are you going to do about it?* Finally, I made my way to the counter. I asked the young lady working behind the register if there might be a place where I could sit in the shade for a bit. I told her I was unfamiliar with the area and just needed a place to sit for a few minutes before my next appointment. I really didn't have an appointment, just planned on popping into the Women's Club, but she didn't have to know that. She told me two blocks south there was a small neighborhood park where I could find some shade. I thanked her, took my water, and headed south.

My forehead was damp by the time I reached the park. I entered and found a faded green wooden bench that was partially shaded by trees and facing the empty playground equipment. A few young mothers and their infants were seated on a blanket on a grassy area that was slightly elevated and completely shaded. They were heavy into mommy conversation. Behind the little group was a row of top-of-the-line strollers. I thought about the $10.99 mint green umbrella stroller that I had purchased when Alex was an infant. My God, what was the year? 1981? I laughed out loud as I recalled it collapsing on our walk, almost swallowing Alex whole because I hadn't locked it into position properly. The gaggle of mothers glanced over at me. I quickly put my hand over my mouth to stifle my giggles. They just as quickly turned their attention back to their discussions of what I could only guess were the topics of breastfeeding, sleeping schedules, and where their child was on the developmental scale. I did not miss those days!

Closing my eyes, I leaned my head back and wished I had brought some aspirin. My head was beginning to throb, most likely from the heat. I rubbed my temples and took a good long swig from the water bottle. Just last week I was sitting in my house, trying to figure out what to make for supper. So much had changed since then.

Savoy, huh? It made me think about Aunt June and Charlie. It made me think back to the day we were at the Coopers while Mom took Charlie to his appointment, and about Jenny, and about all the sadness.

1963

Fourteen

"Jenny, sweetie, talk to me," pleaded Mrs. Cooper in desperation.

I bolted from the living room and ran as fast as my legs could carry me down the short hallway and into our bedroom. I stopped, frozen. All I could see was Mrs. Cooper on her knees, leaning into our tiny closet. The accordion style partition that served as our closet door was pulled back about three quarters of the way. I couldn't see what Mrs. Cooper was seeing, and my feet wouldn't move.

"Oh, my poor, poor girl, tell me what's happened! Can you tell me?" Mrs. Cooper asked frantically. "Is anything broken? Where are you bleeding? Where's the blood coming from? Oh dear, oh, dear!"

I finally found my voice along with my legs, "What's wrong, what's happened?" I screamed, climbing on top of Jenny's bed to see over Mrs. Cooper and into the closet. Jenny was curled up on her left side, knees to her chest, hands clutching her sweater to her mouth. Her knees were bloodied, and she was only wearing one shoe. Her green sweater, the one she wore so proudly for picture day, was torn at the sleeve. She was rocking back and forth. "Mrs. Cooper, what's wrong with her? Is she sick? Jenny, what's wrong with you?" I yelled.

"Ellen, dear, that's not helping. Maybe we should call an ambulance."

No sooner had Mrs. Cooper said ambulance when Jenny wailed, "Noooooooo!"

"Alright, sweetheart, alright, it's okay. You're okay. We won't call if you don't want us to. I promise. *Shhhh...* it's going to be alright. You're safe now. Everything's okay," Mrs. Cooper reassured Jenny in a soothing voice. "Ellen, get her some water and bring a washcloth. Hurry!"

I ran into the kitchen and grabbed a juice glass off the shelf, filled it from the kitchen tap, and carried it sloshing back into the bedroom. I then turned around and got a washcloth from the linen closet and brought it to Mrs. Cooper.

"Dear, get the washcloth wet with warm water," she said as she softly rubbed Jenny's forehead with her fingertips. "Jenny dear, do you think you can sit up and drink some water?"

I came back after I had done as instructed. "Is she going to be alright?" I asked.

"I don't know. Jenny, can you talk to me? Can you tell us what's happened?" she asked softly. Just then I heard what sounded like someone coming through the back door.

"Hello? Anyone here?" I heard my mother call out.

I ran to meet her as she was placing her handbag on the kitchen table and carrying baby Kendall on her hip. My brother Jack was tagging behind.

"Mom! Mom! It's Jenny! Something's happened to Jenny!" I pointed to the bedroom.

"What? What are you talking about?" She handed me my little brother and raced toward the bedroom.

Jack and I followed her and stood at the doorway. "What's she done now?" asked Jack.

"Jane, what happened, what's wrong with Jenny?" Mom said to Mrs. Cooper in a panic as she crawled into the closet and took Jenny up in her arms.

"Annie, I don't know, I really don't know what happened. She left my house to get some board games and change her clothes. After some time, we realized she'd been gone for far too long, and that's when we came looking for her. This is how we found her."

My mother sat on the closet floor for the better part of an hour cradling my sister. Jenny almost seemed catatonic. When Mom tried to move her, she would begin to wail. The mention of a doctor or ambulance set Jenny into uncontrollable wailing. So, Mom just held her.

Mrs. Cooper had long since gone home. Mom had ordered me to feed Kendall and get him ready for bed. I did what I was told, then made peanut butter and jelly sandwiches for Jack and me. We ate them in front of the television.

Mom was still in the bedroom when Dad came through the front door. It startled me because we always heard his car pull up to the carport. I realized then that Dad had gotten a ride home because Mom needed the car today. "What are you guys doing, and why was this shoe left in the yard?" Dad asked, parking his briefcase on the floor, taking off his hat and overcoat. Jack and I just stared at each other because we weren't sure what to say.

"Uh, I think it's Jenny's shoe. Mom's with Jenny. Something happened," I said, using my thumb to point in the direction of the bedroom.

"Christ!" was all he said as he walked in that direction.

Jack and I looked at each other again. We could hear their voices through the bedroom door. They were in there for quite a while before they both came out, without Jenny.

"How's she doing?" I asked. Mom looked so tired. Big dark circles had formed under her eyes. She looked so thin. Dad had his arm around her shoulder.

"I don't know if she's alright or not. She's had a terrible scare. Of what, I don't know. I'm keeping her home from school tomorrow, just to be sure. Maybe take her to see the pediatrician," Mom said wearily. She began to cry. Dad held her tight and patted her back. "Charlie, and now this," she sobbed.

"Charlie. What about Charlie?" I asked.

Dad looked up and said, "Kids, Charlie's extremely sick. Aunt June didn't get good news today."

"He's going to die, isn't he?" I asked.

"Yes, Ellen, he is. But we've got to be strong. We've all got to be strong for him, for Aunt June, for Uncle Max. They're going to need us."

"And Jenny, what about Jenny?" I said through my tears.

"Well, we'll have to be strong for Jenny, too," he said.

My bottom lip began to tremble. Everything bad that could happen was happening. I just wanted it all to stop. "Mom, did Jenny say what happened?"

"She said she fell in the driveway, that someone was chasing her."

Mom wiped her eyes with the backs of her hands. Dad handed her his handkerchief, the thing my dad always carries in his pocket, along with his keys and loose change. Mom took the handkerchief and blew her nose. She took a breath and stood up a bit straighter.

"Who? Who did she think was chasing her?" I asked.

"She said she doesn't know, Ellen. All I know is something scared her badly. We've just got to give her time."

"She's probably just making it all up to get attention. I'll bet she just tripped," Jack said without an ounce of compassion.

"I don't think she's making it up, Jack. You two get ready for bed. I'm going to have you skip your baths tonight," she said, making her way to the kitchen. "And, Ellen, your sister has had a fright, so leave her be. She needs to sleep, okay?"

"Okay," I said.

"Be quiet going into your room. I'll be there in a moment to say goodnight. I'm going to check on Kendall."

"Mom, do you think something really bad happened?"

"I don't know. I really don't know."

"I think it did, Mom, I really think it did."

I stood at the bedroom door for a full minute, my hand lingering on the doorknob. I didn't want to go in. I wasn't tired, I was just sad, I guess. Bad things happen to people all the time, but our family seemed to be in a constant state of sorrow. Both Jack and Charlie were always sick, Mom was always unhappy, Dad was always at work, and Jenny, well, Jenny was always angry. No, I didn't want to go in.

Just then, I heard Dad behind me, clearing his throat. I knew that that was my cue to move it. I turned the knob and entered the room. The moonlight shone through curtains, and I could see the shadowy branches of our oak tree out front. Our little radio was on, the volume at just a whisper and playing a familiar song, but I couldn't think of the title. I walked slowly to my bed and sat on the edge, listening to my sister's breathing. I couldn't tell if she was asleep. She didn't move. She was curled up on her right side, facing away from me, toward the closet. That same closet that just a little while ago she was found in, huddled and scared. I just sat there. Finally, I got up off the bed and unzipped my puppy pillow and pulled out my pajamas. Jenny and I had been given bed pillows to keep our jammies in last Christmas by our grandmother who lived in Macomb. My pillow had the face of a puppy, Jenny's was a cat. I laughed when she opened hers because Jenny hated cats, was deathly afraid of cats. Once she darted up the Pattersons' swing set because a cat came into the yard. She hung off the top of the metal A-frame, screaming her head off for someone to come get that cat. Her screams scared the cat so much that it raced across the street between the houses and was never seen again. Jenny doesn't use her pajama pillow. In fact, I don't even know what she did with it.

I quietly pulled my nightgown over my head and got into bed. I laid there, staring up at the dark ceiling. Just listening. I could faintly hear the train coming down the tracks. Its familiar whistle came about the same time each night. Then came the radio station's jingle. "WLS in Chicago," it sang out. Still, no movement from Jenny. I know Mom told me not to bother her, but that was like telling a bee to stay away from an open soda pop bottle at a picnic.

"Jenny? Jenny, you awake?" I whispered.

No response.

"Jenny, are you okay?" I asked.

No response.

"What happened, Jenny?"

No response.

"You can tell me. I promise I won't tell anybody," I said in the dark. "I promise, I swear."

No response.

"I know something happened. You didn't just fall. Who was it? Who chased you? Was it Stevie? Did he do something, or was it somebody else?"

Stevie was an older kid that lived up the street and was a bit of a bully. He would hide behind the corner of a house, a row of bushes, or a car, and scare the devil out of you. He was really a wimp and probably wouldn't hurt anybody, but he could be a pest.

"Jenny?"

No response.

It was no use. She was either asleep or wasn't talking,

period. I rolled on my back and resumed staring at the ceiling. *She must be asleep*, I told myself.

Just then, a soft coo of an owl or some other feathered friend could be heard outside the window, softly, almost as if it was saying good night.

"Goodnight, little bird," I said.

"I hate birds," whispered Jenny.

Fifteen

The coolness of the shaded bench helped ease the throbbing in my head. However, the sun had risen ever so slightly, exposing my left side to its hot Georgia tentacles. I had a feeling that if I didn't get up and move in a few minutes, I'd look like half a lobster. I opened my eyes and looked straight at the glaring solar beast. Its burning rays proved too much for me. It won! I picked myself up and made my way out of the park.

I pulled up Google maps on my phone for directions to the Brunswick Women's Society. I was elated that according to the map, it was no more than a fifteen-minute walk from where I was standing. It wasn't quite noon, and I was hoping someone would be there, or, even better, that someone could give me some information about Mrs. Caldwell. Anything at all. True to the map's guidance, I found myself standing in front of a three-story stone building, with an enormous set of steps leading up to an enormous set of double doors. It was as if the building was saying "I am important!" Just to the right of the steps was a small bronze plaque that read *The Brunswick Women's Society, Est. 1971, Glynn County, Georgia.* It made me smile. Someone who made the decision regarding the plaque obviously didn't take scale into consideration or just plain didn't care. *Oops*, I thought. That could very well have been Madeline Caldwell since she was the association's founder, if I remembered correctly. Then I thought, *No way she made that decision. That lady paid attention to details.*

I made my way up the steps and kept my fingers crossed that someone would be there. A small sign on the left read *Ring Bell for Assistance*, and under it looked to be some sort of an intercom device with a small white button. I pushed it. I waited. I pushed it again. I waited. I pushed it for the third time. Nothing. I turned around feeling defeated and began making my way down the steps. I was almost to the sidewalk when I heard a voice say, "Canna help ya?"

Almost twisting myself into a pretzel and practically losing my balance, I managed to make it back up the steps. "Oh! Oh yes, yes you can! Oh, my goodness, I'm so glad I caught you!" I said breathlessly. There was an awkward pause as I realized whoever was on the other end of the intercom was waiting for me to explain myself. "I'm so sorry, I'm hoping to speak with someone who might have known Mrs. Caldwell, Mrs. Madeline Caldwell. Uh, my name is Ellen, Ellen Williams, and, well, Mrs. Caldwell left me her house,"

I simply blurted out.

Once again, there was a longer than normal pause.

"Are you there?" I asked.

"Yes, I'm here. Come in. I'll meet ya shortly," said a voice that sounded like a breathless Scarlet O'Hara from *Gone with the Wind*.

The click of the door announced it was unlocked. I entered with renewed hope.

The interior was lovely. There must have been eight large crystal vases filled with creamy pink and white peonies adorning French provincial tables. There were large gold-framed mirrors suspended above two huge fireplaces, and dusty rose damask draperies dressed the floor-to-ceiling windows. A Persian rug of golds, creams, browns, and pinks finished the overall look. At the end of the room was a beautiful spiral staircase that seemed to magically disappear from view, depending on where you were standing. The mistress of ceremonies was the massive cut-glass chandelier that hung dead center from this twenty-foot-tall ceiling. There was no way I would stand under that thing. It reminded me so much of the chandelier in the Caldwell foyer that I wondered if Madeline had been responsible for the interiors in both the house and women's club. I walked around the light fixture while looking up, which was dumb because I swear to God it made me dizzy like those damn teacups at Disney World. I thought I was going to be sick.

"Ms. Williams?" came a soft, southern voice behind

me.

I stopped spinning and turned to the voice. Standing a few feet away from me was a striking elderly lady. I guessed that she was maybe in her late seventies. She was a slender woman, impeccably dressed in a pale pink silk shirt, white linen jacket, and camel-colored slacks. Her hair was light, almost honey blond, perfectly coiffed into a short bob. She wore a braided gold necklace around her aging neck and a matching bracelet on her wrist. If I didn't know better, I would swear she was wearing a pair of Marc Jacobs gold slingback shoes. *You go, girl*, I thought.

"Yes, hello, I'm Ellen Williams," I said, extending my hand. "And you are?"

"I'm Claudia Rosemont," she said with a smile. "I'm current president of our society."

"Oh, I hit the jackpot, the president. Wow! It's nice to meet you. I hope this isn't too much of an imposition, but I really hope you can help me. I tried phoning your club, but I wasn't able to reach anyone, and there was no answering machine to leave a message," I said, trying to explain myself at lightning speed.

"Oh, heavens, I keep meaning to have that fixed," she said putting her hands together so that the tips of each manicured finger united. "It seems to have gone on the fritz last week, and I keep meaning to have someone look at it. I've gotta make a mental note to take care of that this afternoon. Please," she said, gesturing for me to take a seat on one of the sofas.

"Thank you. Well, I've been out talking to some other folks in your beautiful town. I thought I would take a chance and see if anyone was in. Did you know Mrs. Caldwell?"

"Oh, my dear, everyone knew Madeline. She is both a legend in our hearts and in this community. Did I hear you correctly? Did you say you have inherited the Caldwell estate, is that correct?"

"Yes, yes I have. Well, not the entire estate, but her house and surrounding property. And for reasons unknown to me or anyone else, for that matter."

"Well, how marvelous for you! Madeline simply loved her home. It is truly a remarkable piece of property."

"Well, it is an extraordinary bequeath. But I haven't the faintest idea why she left it to me. You see, I don't know Mrs. Caldwell or Judge Caldwell. I've never met them, I'm not a long distant relative. There seems to be no connection that I can find, other than the fact that just this morning I learned that she may have lived at one time in Savoy, Illinois. That's right outside my hometown of Champaign and where an aunt still lives. Judge Caldwell and Mrs. Caldwell were about the same age as my parents. However, I don't know if that has any bearing on anything. So, I guess you can say I'm playing amateur detective and trying to uncover the mystery of Mrs. Caldwell's actions."

"Well, then, how did the lawyer know for sure that you're the right Ellen Williams? That seems like a pretty common name, no offense, dear?"

I laughed. "No offense taken, but a good question.

Mr. Carmichael, Mrs. Caldwell's lawyer, provided me with evidence that confirmed I was the intended recipient: a photograph of me, taken just a couple of years ago."

"Oh! Well, I guess that would be proof. So, you're hoping I can tell you something about Madeline that might fill in some blanks?" she asked.

"Well, yes, if you can. I understand if you don't feel comfortable sharing. But I thought I would try since her nephew indicated that her women's club might be a good place to find some information."

"Aw, Dr. McGaffey. Now, there's a dashing young man!" she said, causing a blush to her cheeks. "He's as handsome as his Uncle Anderson."

"So, the judge was a bit of a heartthrob, huh?" I said with a mischievous grin and wink.

"Oh, my, yes, he was. The ladies in this community would buzz around him like flies near a jam pot. However, he only had eyes for Madeline, that's for sure. There were hearts broken all over Georgia when Anderson came back home with a Yankee bride on his arm. Why, I can remember my sister Iris, who was a few years older than me, God rest her soul, wailed when she got the news that young Anderson had gone and gotten himself married. She fancied herself the next Mrs. Caldwell, but, well, that didn't happen," she said with a shrug.

"I've seen photographs and a painted portrait of the judge. He was quite distinguished looking."

"That he was, as was Madeline. She was a beauty. The young ladies of the town wanted to hate her, but," she said with a soft chuckle, "they just couldn't. She was just too likeable. Hardly an unkind word did you hear uttered from her lips. She was beautiful, quiet, and reserved, but with strong convictions about what was right and what was wrong. I think she and the judge shared more than just their love for one another, but a strong sense of justice, fairness, and courage to take a stand, even if it wasn't always the most popular. Madeline spoke out quietly but firmly on issues such as civil rights, women's rights, and children's rights. She would speak her mind without raising her voice or getting into arguments with others who didn't share her views. She was practical in her approach, usually asking detractors, just for a moment, to put themselves in others' shoes. I admired her. She was a great lady and we all miss her very much."

"What about photographs of her? I'm sure you ladies have had dozens of pictures taken over the years of your club and social events. I ask because I can't seem to find a single one of Madeline in her younger years."

"Funny you mention that. Yes, we have many photo albums and newspaper and magazine articles with pictures of our members highlighting organizational achievements. However, Madeline had a strict rule, absolutely no photographs were to be taken of her. We always thought that strange, seeing how most of us loved having our picture taken. But not Madeline. She shied away from the camera. We just chalked it up as Madeline's peculiarity. We all respected her greatly and wanted to honor her privacy if that's what she wanted."

Did she ever talk about her past, her upbringing, or her family?" I asked.

"Mmm... no, not that I can remember. I think the rumor was that she was orphaned at a young age. We were all terrible gossips, always looking for fault of character. Looking back on it, I should feel a bit ashamed of participating in that kind of behavior," she said, looking as if she was deep in thought over a past transgression. "But," she stated, coming back to the conversation, "somehow we knew that Madeline's past was a topic best left alone. I can't really explain it. We ladies could be vicious when it came to character assassinations. Madeline seemed fragile in some respects and incredibly strong in others. Plus, if I'm to be perfectly honest, if folks had any sense, they knew better than to go and make enemies of the judge's wife."

"Probably wise," I stated. "Did she have a particular group of friends she socialized with more than others?"

"Let me think. We all mainly socialized with her outside the club at charity events or holiday suppers. I know the judge and Madeline occasionally dined with some of his colleagues and their wives, but not often. I don't think they spent a great deal of time with one particular couple more than another. They truly enjoyed just being together, spending time with one another. However, wait—there was a friend of hers, if I remember correctly, that she spent time with, but she wasn't one of our members. Sometimes I would see Madeline shopping or having lunch with her. Let me think, what was her name? Evelyn? Yes, Evelyn. But I'm afraid I don't remember her last name. I believe Madeline said she had lived just outside of town and they had been friends back in Chicago. Oh! Well, I guess I did know a piece of her past after all. I don't even know if this Evelyn is still alive. I haven't seen her in an awfully long time. I don't even remember seeing her at Madeline's funeral.

"Do you remember anything else about her? Maybe her appearance, age, anything?" I pushed on.

"Well, let's see. She looked to be about the same age as Madeline and was tall and thin. The few times I saw them together, her friend was wearing a hat of some sort, so I couldn't tell you hair color or style. She was a smart dresser, if I recall. Like I said, I only saw them together just a couple times in all the years I had known Madeline. I tell ya who might know more about Madeline's friend is her nephew, Dr. McGaffey. He might know more about her."

I was surprised when his name came up again. I thought that if he knew of this friend of his aunt's, he would have mentioned her. That seemed strange, but no stranger that this whole bizarre situation.

"Oh, Mrs. Rosemont, you just might have given me another clue to search," I said.

"Claudia, oh dear! I'm so sorry to interrupt, but you have a telephone call," said a rather short but rotund woman in a squeaky, child-like voice who appeared out of nowhere.

"Mrs. Williams, may I introduce Miss Gladys Slaughter? Gladys, this is Ellen Williams. Gladys is our sergeant-at-arms," she said, turning back to me.

"So nice to meet you," I said, standing up to shake her hand.

"Let me take this call, I'll be right back. Gladys, you worked with Madeline, didn't you? Maybe you can help Mrs. Williams out a bit. She's the new owner of Caldwell estate," she said as she exited the room to take her call.

Gladys's eyes got as big as saucers. "Oh, you don't say! Well, how wonderful! Why yes, I knew Madeline well," she said, clapping her hands together and smiling like a child who was anticipating a sweet treat.

Gladys had to be in her eighties and no more than five feet tall. She had a wide, but kind face. Her dark, curly gray hair resembled steel wool. Her rather round, shapeless body was attached to a thick fleshy neck. She wore a mid-thigh-length multicolored tunic that made her look as if a bouquet of brightly colored spring flowers had just exploded all around her. The wardrobe was completed with white polyester pants and chunky tan sandals.

"Then maybe you could tell me a little bit about Madeline! I would appreciate anyone's help," I said.

"We loved Madeline! I miss her. She was the salt of the earth. Just the salt of the earth."

"That's what I'm hearing from everyone I've talked to. I really wish I could have known her. She sounds like a remarkable human being."

Gladys's face took on a puzzled look. "You didn't know her?"

"No, not at all." And I began filling in what blanks I could for Gladys.

"Well, my goodness, that's quite a story," she said. "We all assumed the entire estate would go to Dr. McGaffey's family. Of course, Madeline did have her fair share of secrets, I would say. But I can assure you, she always had a good reason for anything she did. She seemed to know just what needed to be done and how it was to be done. Whether it was who to invite for the children's cancer research dinner or who should be master of ceremonies for our annual Brunswick Fourth of July parade. She always had impeccable taste and keen insight into things."

"Mrs. Slaughter…"

"Oh heavens, call me Gladys. Mrs. Slaughter was my mother. I never married, dear. And just between you and me, I think my mother wished she hadn't either. My father liked his gin more than he liked her, if you know what I mean," she said tipping an imaginary nip to her mouth.

"Okay, Gladys," I said with a grin. I really liked this woman. "Mrs. Rosemont was telling me of a friend of Madeline's named Evelyn that she'd see her with from time to time. She said this woman wasn't one of your club ladies, and she thinks they may have been friends back when Madeline was in Chicago. Would you know anything about this woman?"

"Evelyn Murray! Yes, I know her. I don't know her well, mind you. She kept to herself. I think she used to work as a bookkeeper or something. I'm not exactly sure. Madeline said she was good with figures."

"Know her, as in, she's still around?" I said with hopeful excitement.

"Why, yes dear, as far as I know. She has to be in her nineties now. I'm almost positive that she's in a nursing home just a few miles from here. In Cypress Mills, I believe."

"Oh, my goodness! That's wonderful news. That's downright great news! Thank you, Gladys!"

"Well, it sounds like Gladys has been able to help a bit," said Mrs. Rosemont, as she drifted back into the room.

"Yes, she was able to tell me a bit about Evelyn, the woman you described with Madeline," I said.

"Really! Why, that's marvelous!"

"Yes, Claudia, don't you remember Madeline's friend, Evelyn Murray?"

"You're right, Gladys, her last name was Murray. Well, see what collective memories will get you?" asked Mrs. Rosemont.

"I can't thank you both enough. I really wasn't sure I'd even find anyone here today, and now you've both helped me with some possible avenues to follow.

Thank you so much for letting me come by unannounced and intrude on your time!" I exclaimed.

"You are quite welcome, my dear," said Gladys.

"We wish you luck in solving the mystery," said Mrs. Rosemont.

"Thanks. If you should remember anything else, anything at all, would you call me? I'll leave you my cell number," I said, rummaging through my purse to find a pen and a scrap of paper.

I quickly wrote down my number and handed it to Claudia Rosemont.

"One more question before I leave: did Madeline ever mention anything about a place she might have lived as a child called Savoy or maybe Champaign?"

Gladys and Claudia looked at each other and shook their heads no.

"That doesn't sound familiar. She never mentioned anything about where she was brought up. In fact, the only mention of her past at all was the day we were talking politics. Remember, Claudia? Most of us are Republicans around here, but not Madeline, she was Democrat. It was the summer before Nixon was elected for the second time. We were at the picnic down at the lake. We'd all had a few cocktails, if I remember correctly. We somehow got on the topic of President Kennedy," said Gladys.

"Oh, yes. But I think we were discussing Jackie Kennedy's sense of style and the men were talking more about politics," said Claudia.

"Maybe so, but Madeline looked very strange and said something about those being the darkest times she could ever remember. That fall of 1963. Wasn't that the year Kennedy was assassinated?" asked Gladys.

Sixteen 1963

"**D**ad, that man just shot him!" I yelled out, totally dumbfounded as I just witnessed live on television the man accused of shooting Kennedy get shot.

"Oh, my God! Ann, get in here, you're not going to believe this! Some guy just shot Oswald! I've got to call the paper!" he shouted as he jumped up and ran to the phone.

Mom came rushing into the living room from the kitchen, carrying a jar of puréed peaches in one hand and Kendall's baby spoon in the other. Jack and Jenny ran into the room as well. I sat frozen, shocked that I had just seen someone get shot. I mean, right then, while I was sitting there. It wasn't a movie; this was for real, and I couldn't move. Dad and I had been sitting together on the living room sofa, watching them bring Lee Harvey Oswald through the basement of the Dallas police station. One minute he was handcuffed and walking between two men, the next he was down.

"What's going on?" Jack asked.

"Shhh!" Mom shushed as she ran over to turn up the TV. It was bedlam on the screen. We heard shouting, and people began running everywhere. The man with the gun had been tackled. The camera seemed to jump around sporadically, making it hard to tell what was going on. We all sat in a trance, watching what would be for the second time in a period of two days a moment in history we would never forget.

"Oswald, I think he killed Oswald," I could hear Dad frantically relaying to whomever was on the other end of the phone. Dad, who was a reporter for our local newspaper *The Courier*, was making sure the paper was aware of what just happened. He had come in late the night before, having spent the better part of the weekend covering the President's assassination. Now this.

"For Christ's sake! What the hell is happening in this country? People are running around with guns killing everybody," Mom said with anger in her voice.

"Do you think he's dead?" Jack asked.

"I hope so. I hope he killed him. He killed Kennedy; he deserves it," Jenny said, void of emotion.

All of us, even Dad, who still had the phone in his

hand, turned to stare at her. It was the first time in a month that Jenny had said much of anything.

On Monday the next week, we tried to go about the business of living life. But sadness blanketed everything like a menacing fog that had seeped into every crevice of my world. It wasn't just what was happening in the nation, but what was happening right here. Charlie wasn't doing well, and Jack was having issues with his kidneys. It looked like my older brother would have to undergo another surgery after the holidays. Mom walked around all the time with dark circles under her eyes. Dad, well, Dad spent most of his time at work. The temperature dropped the night before and the wind had picked up. Though the calendar said it was still autumn, it felt like winter.

"Girls, it's cold out there this morning. Make sure you bundle up. You might want to wear slacks today to keep your legs warm," Mom called out to Jenny and me as we were preparing for school. "Let's move, your brother has had a rough night."

I had heard Jack call out for Mom in the middle of the night. Then bath water could be heard running in the wee hours of the morning. Sometimes the only thing that would ease his pain was a warm bath. I didn't quite understand exactly what was wrong with him, but I did know that his pain could be excruciating based on his cries that sounded like a wounded animal. When he was well, Jack could be your typical older brother—annoying, funny, and mischievous. He once chased me around the cul-de-sac with a black snake that he found near the train tracks. He had somehow managed to get the snake to curl itself around an old aluminum curtain rod. Jack ran behind me, jabbing the rod in my back and laughing like a crazy person. He only dropped the rod when the damn thing slithered closer to his own hand. Jack never got in trouble. I mean never! Mom defended him no matter what. His illness was always his Get Out of Jail Free card. But Jenny and I really didn't mind all that much. I wouldn't trade places with him, no matter how many free passes I were given.

Jenny and I braced ourselves as the first wave of icy winds found our faces. I pulled my earmuffs firmly in place and adjusted my scarf over my mouth. We knew it was going to feel like a much longer walk to school today. But then, it started snowing.

"It's snowing! It's snowing!" I squealed, ignoring the brutal wind whipping strands of hair in my face as I tried catching the first snowflakes of the season on my tongue.

Jenny didn't respond. She kept her head down and kept walking. She didn't appear to be interested in the first snowfall. In fact, Jenny hadn't been interested in much of anything since "that night." That's how Mom and Dad always described it when referring to the incident.

Give her time, she had a scare "that night."

Jenny has become so much quieter since "that night."

Do you think she needs to talk to someone, maybe a counselor, about "that night"?

Jenny wouldn't speak of "that night." I tried on several occasions to get her to talk about it. She finally told me she'd punch me in the face if I mentioned it again. I believed her, so I shut up.

"What do you want for Christmas, Jenny?" I asked as I watched the icy plumes of my own breath appear and then disintegrate.

"I don't know."

"I want the new Midge doll, you know, Barbie's friend. And I want some new Barbie clothes and maybe a new Barbie case. My old one's ripping apart."

"Aren't you a little old to be playing with Barbies?" Jenny remarked.

"Nope," I simply stated as I continued catching snowflakes on the tip of my tongue.

"C'mon, you must want something," I continued to press.

"Yeah, I want you to stop asking me what I want."

"You don't mean that; you're always the first to let Mom know what you want for Christmas."

Grabbing my coat sleeve and practically twirling me 180 degrees she screamed, "I DON'T WANT *ANYTHING* FOR CHRISTMAS BUT TO BE LEFT ALONE!"

"Okay, okay! You don't have to get all mad about it. I was only asking," I said, yanking my arm back from her grip.

We continued walking the rest of the way in silence. We parted once we entered the school. Jenny turned right, I turned left at the top of the steps. No words were spoken.

By the time school ended and the dismissal bell rang, there were about four-to-five inches of snow on the ground, and it was still snowing. I grabbed my coat from the cloakroom and tried putting it on while running for the door.

"Slow down!" yelled Mrs. Erikson, who was standing just outside the doorway of her third-grade class and directly across from my own classroom. Denise Jefferson, one of my good friends, was neck-and-neck with me. We were like wild ponies, just itching to let it rip. We both giggled, but slowed down a bit doing a half-walk, half-run down the hall. I could see through the window at the end of the hall that the snow was still falling. I couldn't wait to get home and play in the snow. The only real joy I had felt in months. We raced down the steps, only to stop short due to a logjam of kids trying to be the first out the door.

"I'm going to build a snowwoman," announced Denise.

"You mean, she'll have boobs," I said laughing at the anticipation of having fun.

"No, silly. My mom would box my ears if I did that. No, I'm just going to make her curvy, put some old sunglasses on her and maybe one of my mom's old floppy beach hats. Maybe use my plastic shovel and pail we always take to the beach as props. She's going to be a summer snowwoman. I'll name her Summer Snow."

I laughed. Denise always had quite the imagination, and I loved her for it.

"Ellen, wait up!"

I could see Jenny coming down the stairs from the opposite hallway. The fifth-grade classes always had to use the other set of stairs to keep the congestion in the halls down. It didn't appear to be working all that well on this snowy afternoon.

"Wait for me in front," she said from across the sea of students. Jenny was smiling. I hadn't seen her smile in a while, and I automatically smiled back.

"Okay, if we ever get out of here!" I yelled over the noise.

The clogged drain of bodies finally busted through the crowded entryway, and we all flew down the "just swept" front steps. Kids were immediately stopping and scooping up fistfuls of snow and blasting each other in the faces before they themselves became targets. Everyone was laughing, screaming, and loving the wet, icy mess.

Denise waved goodbye as she dodged a snowball coming her way. I watched her as she made her way down the sidewalk and turned left toward home. "Have fun with Summer Snow!" I yelled.

She answered me by turning in a snowy swirl and giving me the thumbs up.

I looked around for Jenny while keeping my eyes out for an errant snowball. I could see her making her way down the steps. She was moving slowly as to keep from colliding with the icy concrete below. "Over here, Jenny!" I said as I made my way toward her.

Billy Kramer was about to throw a major snowball our way when Jenny said, "If you do it, you die." Billy, with his floppy mop of hair in his eyes, stopped, grinned, and let it fly, hitting Jenny in the gut. That's all it took. Jenny threw down her books and ran after him. He zigzagged around the flagpole, laughing the whole time, and daring Jenny to do something about it.

"Come on, Jenny, I dare ya," he taunted.

Jenny stepped back a few feet, and, with lightning speed, scooped up two fistfuls of snow, formed the most perfect snowball, and delivered it upside Billy's head in less than five seconds. It literally knocked Billy off his feet.

"Not so tough now, are you, Billy?" Jenny said with a laugh. I ran up behind her, lending assistance if needed. But Billy just laid there laughing. And then we all were laughing.

Jenny picked up her books that she had scattered across the snowy ground and said, "Let's go, Ellen, I think we're done here."

My feet and hands were cold, and I wasn't looking forward to walking home. We no sooner hit the parking lot when Jenny and I saw our father, standing outside his open car door, waiting. Something was wrong. We both stopped.

"Charlie's dead," I said.

"Or Jack," Jenny whispered.

We looked at each other with dread. It wasn't just the icy temperatures keeping us frozen in our tracks. That spontaneous moment of sheer joy for the first snowfall dissipated like the snowflakes themselves hitting the ground.

"Dad, what's wrong? Is Charlie dead? What happened?" I asked as we finally reached the car, my words spilling out like frosty clouds.

Dad stood silently, like a statue in a blizzard. His hat was firmly on his head, his glasses fogged up so much you couldn't see his eyes, and his mouth was completely covered by his gray wool scarf that was wrapped around the collar of his trench coat.

I had never seen my dad cry until that day. "Girls, girls," he choked up as he reached for both of us and pulled us close. He began to sob. "I'm afraid Charlie's gone, kids." Suddenly, the whiteout of the afternoon turned black. The light turned off and we were suffocating in sorrow. "Get in," Dad said as he finally untangled his arms from around us.

The car ride home took only a few short minutes, but everything seemed to move in slow motion. I didn't want to go into the house. I didn't want to face all the sadness that would fill the house for who knows how long. Jenny sat motionless and silent next to me in the back seat. We turned down our street. Through the fog of the car window, an unfamiliar object in the yard across the street caught my eye. The Jamesons' house was for rent. After what happened there just a month or so earlier, it wasn't surprising to see the red *For Rent* sign. Henry Jameson supposedly snapped and, in a rage, shoved his father so hard that it resulted in his death and then turned around and shot himself. I overheard Mr. Cooper tell Dad one afternoon shortly after it happened that a lot of men are never quite the same after war. That war does crazy things to a man's head. Nobody really knows why he did it. And his wife, well, she just kind of vanished. I doubt they'll ever find her. I just wondered what ever happened to Bird.

Seventeen

The rain began early. Lightning illuminated the morning sky. Raindrops picked up speed, pelting the French doors that led to the patio. The occasional roll of thunder with its perfectly choreographed timing after each bolt of lightning was strangely reassuring. It was predictable. It was as it should be.

The storm didn't wake me. I'd been awake for a few of hours, even though it was barely 8:00 a.m. I had spent the last several hours staring at the ceiling, hoping sleep would come. It didn't. I finally surrendered, threw off the afghan, and got up to make coffee. "C'mon, girl. I guess we can get you some breakfast," I said. Following me into the kitchen, Lilly sat on her haunches, tail swishing, waiting for breakfast. I envied her eagerness for something as simple as a can of dogfood. Well, maybe

165

I feel the same way about a good glass of wine after a particularly hard day. "I'm coming, girl, hold on," I assured her.

After feeding Lilly and dashing outside for her morning potty break, battling torrential raindrops with an umbrella and wearing a kitchen towel over my head, I was able to return to the comfort of the couch and my coffee. Lilly, having been fed and watered, jumped up next to me with partially wet paws and laid her damp head in my lap. She looked at me with such unconditional love that I almost cried. "I know, girl. I love you, too."

Though the storm didn't seem to be losing its energy, it somehow comforted me. I hoped it would end sometime soon. After my conversations with Claudia and Gladys, I decided to skip lunch in town yesterday and just come back to my home base. I was hot, sticky, and tired. Once home, I poured myself a cold glass of iced tea, put my feet up, and began searching for Evelyn Murray. How hard could it be to find her? It wasn't. A few keystrokes on my laptop brought me to the website of Cypress Mills Nursing Facility, including a map and phone number. I called. My questions were simple: was there an Evelyn Murray presently living at the facility, and could she have visitors? The answers on the other end of the phone were yes and yes. I was told that due to HIPAA privacy regulations, they were not allowed to discuss her medical condition. However, a nurse did tell me that Evelyn was ninety-one years of age and understandably easily exhausted, but generally she was more alert in the mornings through mid-afternoon.

I was hoping I could get there today. So, I crossed my fingers that the storm would let up a bit so I could go. I sat there with Lilly feeling a sense of contentment even with all the turbulence going on outside. A kind of peace had come over me. Something I hadn't felt in, well, so long I couldn't remember. I didn't realize that I needed this, whatever "this" was. A few months before I received the first notification from the lawyer regarding Mrs. Caldwell's estate, I had grown extremely anxious. I was angry, sad, and constantly searching for something. No one in the family knew that I had sought counseling. To me, it had always been something I had regarded as weak or something for folks who couldn't solve their own problems. I was unhappy in my life, my marriage, my future. I didn't even know why. Leaving Dan had even crossed my mind. I loved him, but I was feeling smothered. I fantasized about picking up and taking off for parts unknown. I was almost there, almost ready to act on it, when Dan got word of possible cancer. Then I felt guilty. What kind of a person was I? I couldn't leave a man with cancer. Then, I felt totally lost. I had to stay; I had to go. Then I got the call verifying ownership of the estate, and I realized I could do both. I could stay, but I could go. Give myself some time to think, while still supporting him, still loving him. Nobody would have to know what was going on inside my mind. I had bought myself a little time, or Mrs. Caldwell had. I reached for my coffee and knocked her photograph off the coffee table onto the floor. "Oh, shit. Sorry, Madeline," I said out loud as I picked it up and placed it back where it was. "I hope you don't mind me calling you Madeline. I feel we've somehow reached that stage in our relationship. You know, Madeline, if you want to send me some kind of a sign, I promise I won't get spooked. It would take more than a few spirits or moving objects to frighten me at this stage of the game," I laughed.

Just then, my phone rang, causing me to practically wet myself. I fumbled in my pocket to retrieve my phone. It was Sharon. "Well, hello, lady!" I said.

"Well, hi. I was going to leave you a message. I didn't think you'd pick up this early. I'm driving out to the lake to check on the house and thought I'd give you a ring. I hope it's not too, too early. This stretch of road on sixty-five is long and boring." Sharon's lake house was nestled in an area known as Nolin Lake. We have spent many summer days anchoring her pontoon in a peaceful cove and floating in the water while holding a red solo cup full of vino.

"Well, I'm up. It's after 9:00 a.m. now, and I've got things I want to get done, that is, if this weather cooperates. We're having a rather nasty little storm here that woke me early. I'm just chilling with Lilly and talking to Mrs. Caldwell," I said with a laugh.

"You're what?"

"Well, I'm not actually talking to her, just her photo. You know, a big house, a thunderstorm, being alone. It makes a person start doing some weird stuff," I laughed. "I'm not running through the halls dragging an axe or anything yet."

"Oh, Lord! You sure you don't need some company?"

"Well, I'd love some, but I'm really okay. Making a bit of progress." I proceeded to tell Sharon what I had thus far accomplished, as minimal as it was. "So, I'm going to see if I can visit the old girl this afternoon. That is, if she even knows her own name. *Heh*, I don't have a lot of room to talk. I can walk from one room to another and not remember what I went in there for in the first place."

"Wow, ninety-one! Good luck!"

"Yep, we shall see. It might just be another dead end, but I have to admit, it's been rather fascinating. All I can do is try, and, of course, without sounding callous, time is really of the essence with Evelyn to try and glean any kind of information from her. Poor soul." Just then, someone was beeping in. "Hold on a minute, Sharon." I looked at the phone and saw Hunter McGaffey's name. "Sharon, can I call you back? It's Mrs. Caldwell's nephew on the line."

"Oh, sure, but you better damn well call me back and tell me everything."

"I promise! I'll give you a full report!" I clicked over to the incoming call.

"Hunter, hello," I answered with just a twinge of skepticism.

"Good morning. I didn't wake you, did I?" asked Hunter.

"Oh, heavens no! Who could sleep with this racket going on?" I said

"No one. We can get some pretty mean storms down here. I wanted to make sure you hadn't lost power or anything. Especially being out there by yourself." His last sentence gave me pause. Should I be worried? I suddenly felt the need to get up and check that the alarm was set, and the doors and windows were locked.

"Could you hold on for just a second?" I asked, trying not to sound fearful in any way.

"Sure."

I even made my way to the pantry. I slowly entered and was relieved to see the cellar door was still bolted. I was letting my imagination get the best of me.

"Ellen, are you there?"

"Uh, yeah, sorry, just thought I heard something, but it was just a branch against the window," I lied trying to recover the conversation without giving away my paranoia. "That's truly kind of you for checking in, but so far we've got power. If it had gone out, I would have been out making a coffee run. Short of a tornado, I would weather any storm for my caffeine."

"Ha, I can relate," he said.

"Listen, Hunter, it's good you called because I was going to give you a call anyway. Your Aunt Madeline, do you remember her having a friend by the name of Evelyn Murray?" I asked.

"Evelyn Murray. Oh gosh, yes, Evelyn or Miss E. as we used to refer to her. Boy, that takes me back a few years. I had totally forgotten about Evelyn. Yes, she and my aunt had been friends for years. I don't think any of us has seen her in years. Gosh, if she's still alive, she must be in her nineties by now," he stated.

"Ninety-one to be exact," I said.

Hunter whistled into the phone. "I really didn't think she was still alive. Aunt Madeline and Uncle Anderson had her over to the house frequently throughout the years. I can't tell you how she and my aunt met. I think maybe they had been friends back in Chicago, but don't quote me on that. She was kind of an odd bird. Seems to me she was an accountant or worked in finance or something. Pretty much kept to herself even when there was a big gathering at the house. You say she's still alive?"

"Uh-huh, just down the road at Cypress Mills Nursing Facility. I found out yesterday from a couple of ladies from your aunt's women's club. I've called the nursing facility, and they told me she's still there. I thought maybe I'd ride out today if the weather cooperates. I have a feeling she might be suffering from dementia at her age and may be of no help whatsoever, but I thought I'd try," I said.

"It's worth a shot. I'd go with you, but I'm scheduled for surgery this afternoon," said Hunter.

"Oh, don't worry about it. It might just be a wild goose chase anyway."

"Hey, listen, I was also calling to see if maybe the girls and I can stop in tomorrow, say around 1:00 p.m., to allow the girls to pay their respects to their aunt. If you already have plans, I understand."

"No, tomorrow would be fine. I'm looking forward to meeting your girls and seeing where the judge and his wife are laid to rest on the property. Why don't you plan on staying for lunch? It won't be anything fancy, but I could use a little company," I replied.

"That would be lovely. Thank you for the lunch invitation. Tomorrow, then, around one o'clock."

"Yes, tomorrow. See you then."

I hung up the phone feeling happy. Maybe what I was feeling was anticipation for doing something new, something different. Whatever it was, I would embrace these positive feelings that had somehow been escaping me lately. I got up off the couch and walked to window. Rain was beading up, forming water droplets against the pane. Each drop seemed to magnetically find another, two becoming one as they made their descent down the glass. My mind began to drift, changing the rain, changing the time.

Eighteen

The snow had accumulated in the crevices of the car's foggy windows. The windshield wipers did little to improve visibility. The five-minute drive from school to home felt like forever. Though the driveway was covered with a blanket of virgin snow, you could feel and hear the crunch of the gravel as the car made its way up the drive, seeking protection of the carport. I sat frozen and not just from the cold. I didn't want to get out. Neither did Jenny.

"Let's go, girls," Dad said as he opened Jenny's car door.

"No," she replied.

"Jenny, come on. It's freezing."

"No!" she said louder.

"Goddammit, Jenny, I don't have time for your shenanigans!" he said, void of patience or emotion. "Ellen, you too, get out!"

I opened the car door, bracing myself for the wind and snow. I didn't want to go into that house either, but I couldn't very well stay in the car and freeze to death. "C'mon Jenny, it's cold out here."

Suddenly, Jenny was out of the car, racing down the driveway, onto the cul-de-sac, and up the street. Without thinking, I took off after her, calling her name.

"Jenny! Jenny! Come back, come back, I need you! Come back, please come back!" I cried. "Please come back, please!" I cried as my foot came out from under me, trying to keep my balance on the snow-covered street. The pavement won. My knees hurt. I could feel the strange mixture of cold and sting. I had torn my trousers clear through, exposing a wet bloody knee. I rolled over and sat in the snow, crying. It started out as a quiet whimper that suddenly turned into an animal cry of despair. Jenny stopped. Through my tears, I could see her breath in the distance as she exhaled. Total anguish on her face. She came back, slowly, as if each step was agony. She dropped to her knees and wrapped her arms around me. There we sat, huddled together in the middle of the street, wet and cold. The snow coming down all around us. Just the two of us. We sat there, mourning the loss of a little boy, drowning in our own sorrow for what had been and what would be. Suddenly, large arms wrapped around both of us. "I know, girls, I know," was all Dad said.

The next two weeks leading up to Christmas weren't easy. Aunt June had come to stay with us. Mom and Dad said it would be a little while, just until she felt strong enough to go home. We watched as she survived on cigarettes and coffee. How do you pretend all is merry and bright when you've just buried your child? There could be no pretending.

"Can I get you anything, June?" Mom asked, trying to untangle the Christmas lights so that they could be hung on the tree. Aunt June shook her head. I was sitting on the sofa next to her, drawing a picture to cheer her up. A car door slammed from across the street. I climbed up on my knees and peered over the sofa, pulling back the living room sheers.

"Somebody's over at the Jamesons' house," I said. Jenny's head snapped up.

"They're probably showing the house," Mom said.

"I wonder if they'll tell the new tenants about the Jamesons?" Dad said.

"Either way, they'll find out soon enough. You can't have had a murder and suicide in a house and keep that quiet," Mom stated.

"Well, maybe whoever rents it can get a discount," Dad said with a chuckle.

"That's not funny, Bob! There's nothing funny about it. What happened in that house was a real tragedy," Mom said.

"You're right, it's not funny. I just thought we needed a little levity," Dad said solemnly.

"Best to change the subject altogether," Mom said

nodding her head sideways in my direction. "Here, this is your job. Put the lights on the tree, please, so the kids can start decorating with the ornaments," she directed Dad.

"Jenny, grab that box of ornaments, and help your sister," ordered Mom.

"I don't feel like decorating the tree," Jenny spat and left the room.

Mom sighed. The permanent dark circles under her eyes made her look as if she hadn't slept in weeks. Any other time, Mom would have gone toe-to-toe with Jenny. But not today. She was just too weary. Kendall had been teething most of the day but was finally quiet, chewing on toy blocks in his playpen. Jack was at a friend's house. I envied Jack being away.

"Okay, Ellen, looks like it's you and me then."

I picked up a box of ornaments. Mom had meticulously wrapped each in tissue paper the year before. I began unwrapping them. Each evoked memories of days gone by. The silver bell from Grandma Sanders, the Santa with his pipe clenched tight in his mouth and an extended belly, the elves in their green-and-red felt hats, dozens of colorful balls, partially covered in fake snow, which we always sprayed at the end of the decorating process. We were never allowed to use tinsel. Mom said it looked cheap, so we always sprayed the tree with fake snow at the end. It gave the tree a soft glow in the nights leading up to Christmas.

We finished the tree and stood back to admire the

beauty that a lighted Christmas tree could bring. However, not even its beauty could lift the spirits of the occupants in this house. Everyone stepped away to begin their evening tasks. Mom retrieved Kendall from the playpen and headed into the kitchen to feed him, Dad went to pick up Jack from his friend's house, and Jenny was sulking in her room, refusing to come out and share in what little joy there was. Only Aunt June remained where she had been, sitting in the exact same spot she had occupied earlier. Now the light of day was gone, only shadows left along with the embers of her cigarette glowing in the dark. I approached her slowly and crawled up next to her on the couch. I reached for her hand. "Aunt June, don't be sad. I guess God needed an extra angel for Christmas."

Nineteen

The storm subsided by noon. A gray overcast remained with just a hint of spitting rain. I could deal with that. According to Google maps, Cypress Hill was on the outskirts of Brunswick, and it would take little time to get there. My plan was to make it there after the whole lunch process took place. I'd been in several nursing homes in the past, and I knew better than to show up at feeding time.

I hopped in the shower and let the steam open my pores. It felt wonderful. I lingered a little longer than I should have, but my body just wouldn't let me move quickly. Afterwards, I did my best to look presentable. I quickly blow-dried my hair, running my hands through my scalp, trying to control the waves so as not to end up with a frizzy mess. I'm not sure why I was even bothering. I threw on my white capri pants, a flowery pink-and-green short-sleeved blouse, and a pair of beige sandals. I applied a little color to my lips and cheeks and even gave my eyelashes a swipe of mascara. *Not too bad for an old married lady*, I thought.

I rummaged in the refrigerator for a quick bite before heading out. I grabbed an apple, a jar of peanut butter, a bottled water, and a block of cheddar cheese off the top shelf. It wasn't exactly gourmet, but it would do. I sliced the apple and allowed myself generous dollops of peanut butter on each slice. I knew I probably looked like a heathen in my gluttonous state, but who cares. I grabbed the saltines off the counter and topped each cracker with a thick slice of cheese. My hunger was ridiculous. Did I eat breakfast? I couldn't even remember. Anyway, who cares? Having inhaled my lunch, I made my way back to the bathroom to brush my teeth. Nothing worse than peanut butter breath.

I grabbed my umbrella from my suitcase and headed out. It was eerily quiet, almost foggy from the precipitation coming off the hot earth. Once in the car, I plugged in the address for the Cypress Mills Nursing Facility and hit "Start Guidance."

"Here we go," I said out loud.

In no time, I was pulling into the facility. I parked the car and began making my way into the front entrance. It looked like so many other nursing homes. It appeared to be all one level, shaped almost like a cross if you were to take an aerial view. The wide front entrance had double automatic doors to accommodate wheelchairs, walkers, or ambulance gurneys, most likely. Not a happy place, but a necessary one. I entered to find a charming front lobby furnished with sofas, wingback chairs, and a big-screen TV over a faux fireplace. It made me smile that they were enjoying a roaring fire in the middle of a Georgia summer. A young woman seated at the reception desk warmly greeted me as I stepped closer.

"Good afternoon, can I help you?"

"Yes, I'm here to see one of your residents, Ms. Evelyn Murray."

"Absolutely. I just need you to sign in, please." She scooted the book closer for my signature.

"Okay, Ms. Williams," she said, glancing at my signature. "Ms. Murray is in room 118. You just head straight down this corridor, turn right just past the nurses' station, and her room will be on the right."

"Thank you."

"My pleasure. Have a nice visit."

I took my time finding her room. I wasn't sure what kind of shape I'd find Evelyn in. When I finally reached room 118, I hesitated. Was I really doing the right thing by bothering this woman? I turned around to leave. *This might be a mistake*, I thought.

"I think she might be dozing a bit; she always takes a little nap after lunch. Go on in, she'll be glad to have some company. Ms. Evelyn doesn't get too many visitors," said a friendly voice behind me. I spun around to see a heavy-set lady in her mid-thirties wearing blue scrubs and carrying a load of what looked to be bed linens. Perhaps a nurse's assistant. I couldn't quite make out what was written on her name tag.

"Oh, really, I just wanted to stop by and say hello. We had a mutual friend," I lied.

"Well, Ms. Evelyn's a character. You'll find that out soon enough. She might be old, but she's more on the ball than most of us. Yep, she's a real character. Don't let me hold you up. Go on. She's feisty, but she don't bite! Ha!"

"You sure? Now you got me a little worried," I said, laughing, but I really meant it.

"Naw, you're good."

"Okay, thanks," I said as I stepped into the room.

Sure enough, Ms. Evelyn was sleeping soundly in her wheelchair by the window as the afternoon sun was just beginning to peak through the clouds. A green blanket had been tucked around her. She looked peaceful. Her head was tilted to one side, her breathing slow and steady. I didn't want to disturb her, so I sat in the only chair in the room, located on the other side of her bed. I watched her as she slept and waited. She had completely white hair, almost like snow. She had a prominent jaw line, with little sagging around her neck and face for her age. She was quite thin, and, though she was in a wheelchair, I would bet she was above average height. Like Mrs. Caldwell, there was something oddly familiar about her. But that's all it was, a familiarity. I was clueless. She slept on. I finally got out my phone and turned the ringer off. I didn't want it to wake her in case someone tried to call. I began checking my messages and emails while Sleeping Beauty dozed.

"Is that what they call one of those smartphones?"

I practically dropped the phone; I was so surprised. Once I got my wits about me, I answered, "Why yes, yes, it is."

"Technology's going to be the death of us all."

"You might be right," I said with a smile.

"That's all you see is the top of everybody's head these days 'cause they're all looking down at their damn phones."

"I'm afraid that's true. We always have a rule in our house, no phones allowed at the dinner table. It's the only time I have my kids' attention," I said with a laugh.

"Hmph…. Well, kids today need to be taught to show more respect."

"Well, I don't disagree," I said. "Uh, Ms. Murray, my name is Ellen, Ellen Williams."

I waited to see if there was any response. A flicker or a twitch. Her face showed nothing.

"I'm from Louisville, Kentucky, but I spent my early years in Champaign, Illinois."

Did I see her blink? I think she blinked. I pressed on, "I'm here today because a special friend of yours brought me here. Madeline Caldwell."

"Madeline's dead."

"Well, yes, I know, Ms. Murray, and I'm sorry for the loss of your friend. I heard you two were awfully close. But, you see, I'm trying to understand why your friend Madeline left me a special gift. I was hoping that you might be able to help me. I've tried finding answers on my own. I've met with her nephew, her lawyer, her minister, and even some of the ladies of her women's club. All of it's led me to you."

"I can't help you."

"Well, you don't even know the gift," I said a little too defensively.

"It doesn't matter. I can't help you," she said emphatically.

I sat and looked at her for a full thirty seconds. I know she wasn't telling me the truth. I didn't think I could explain putting a ninety-one-year-old women in a chokehold, so I had to come up with another tactic.

"Ms. Murray, Madeline left me her estate. Her beautiful home and the surrounding grounds. I can't, no, I won't, accept a gift of that magnitude without understanding the reason behind it. It doesn't belong to me, and, out of respect to Madeline and her family, I must return it to them. I want to honor her wishes, but I can't if I don't understand them. If you can't help me, I have no choice but to go to her lawyer and have him place the property back into her estate for the family. You probably knew your friend better than anyone, except maybe the judge. Can you tell me this, is this what she really wanted?"

She stared back at me. I could see the wheels turning

behind those dark eyes. She was weighing her options, the crafty old gal. This lady was savvy. She hadn't survived this long without knowing how to navigate her world.

"If Mae left you her house, it was meant for you."

"But why, why?"

"Ms. Williams," she said with a sigh, "things happen for reasons we don't fully understand. Accept her gift and move on."

"I can't, Ms. Murray. I wasn't raised that way."

"I know you weren't, my dear."

"You know, don't you?" I asked.

She looked at me for several seconds and finally said, "Yes, I do, dear. But then, you probably know more than you think you do," as she tapped the side of her head with her long, crooked finger. She refused to say more. Her actions reminded me of when I had a drink with Judy and she had tapped her head just as Evelyn did, and told me I might hold the key to this mystery.

I couldn't have been more frustrated leaving that afternoon. What on earth was that all about? Hell, I was more confused than when I started. I felt like screaming. I was tired of these damn games. I was ready to call it quits. First thing Monday morning I would see Jimmy and tell him to do whatever the hell he needed to do to transfer all of this out of my name and back to the Caldwell estate. It was a beautiful gift, an extraordinary gift, an un-fucking-believable gift. But it wasn't mine. It should never have been mine. I have no earthly idea what her motives were. Mrs. Caldwell may or may not have been trying to buy her way into the gates of heaven with this act of contrition. Maybe she was just some eccentric old bird that closed her eyes one day, and decided just for kicks, she'd leave her most prized possession to a total stranger. *Who the fuck knows?* It was time for me to go home. I'd had my fun playing amateur sleuth. It didn't matter anymore. I needed to go home. I needed to be with Dan, to be with my family.

On the way home, I called Dan, then I called Mia, and then I called Alex. I just wanted to hear everyone's voices. I needed to make sure my family was okay. I wanted them to know I was okay and that I loved them. I assured them all that I would be home sometime next week. I just had to take care of a few things before I left. I realized that this house, for all its beauty, seemed a lonely place. And, though Judge and Mrs. Caldwell seemed to have a wonderful relationship by all accounts, I feared this house became more of an asylum for them rather than a real home. I don't know. I obviously will never know. I had resigned myself to that.

"Hey, lady, how was your afternoon?" I asked Lilly as I entered the foyer. "I'll bet it was a hell of a lot more productive than mine. C'mon, let's get you outside. Let me get on my tennis shoes first."

The afternoon had been so frustrating. No amount of pleading would break that woman. I needed to breathe. The grass was still damp from the morning storm. I walked Lilly to the water's edge. The ducks were on the far side of the pond happily going about their business. Lilly was now used to seeing them and no longer tried to drag me over. I let her lead me around, and I readily followed. I figured for the next few days I would just enjoy being there and remember the tranquility of the place. I was sure people would think I was crazy walking away from a property like this, but it wasn't mine. And I certainly didn't need the money. Dan and I had done quite alright for ourselves. We worked hard and had never asked anyone for anything. We managed to put two kids through college and grad school, owned a nice home, still had successful businesses, and each had a good retirement plan. We had what we needed. That was more than enough.

"Okay, lady, mama needs a glass of wine. Let's go, we'll get you fed, too."

I filled Lilly's bowl and poured myself a glass of Chardonnay. It was still hot outside, but I wasn't in the mood to be indoors. I took my glass out to the front porch and plopped myself on the porch swing. I kicked off my shoes, took a long sip, and laid my head back. It felt wonderful letting the alcohol take effect—that numbing feeling that makes your insides glow. I could hear the cicadas and feel a warm breeze begin to pick up. It was an awfully pretty place. "I'm going to miss you," I said to the house.

Suddenly, I sat up. Wait, did she mean to say that name? Was that an error on her part? Did she mean to say that name? And, before I could take another sip of wine, a piece of the puzzle fell into place.

1963

Twenty

I awoke to the sound of Mom and Dad talking—
well, whispering. My bedside clock said it was
almost 11:30 p.m. *That's strange, everybody's usually asleep
by now.* I pulled the covers down and listened. Was
Jack having another episode? I didn't hear the bath
water running or him moaning, but they were
definitely awake and whispering behind their
bedroom door. It sounded different—they were
talking in rushed, short sentences. Jenny was asleep. I
could see the covers move ever so slightly as she lay
breathing. I quietly got out of bed and tiptoed to my
closed bedroom door. I put my ear up against it and
listened. I couldn't quite make out exactly what they
were saying. Something about a bus leaving at 12:45. *I
don't remember Mom or Dad mentioning that either one of
them was going anywhere.* I gently turned the doorknob
and peaked out. The lights were on. I quietly slipped
out and down the hall. I stopped. At first, I didn't
recognize the woman standing in our living room. She
just stood there, all alone. She was wearing a long

brown coat with a wide circular collar, fastened all the way up to her neck with large black buttons. Her dark, shoulder-length hair was partially covered by a red beret. Her gloved hand clutched a battered suitcase and the other held a pocketbook and a tissue that she would raise to her eyes. She'd been crying, that was obvious. She hadn't seen me enter. I was so surprised to see this woman just standing in our living room. I was a little scared of her because of all the rumors I'd heard, but she looked so afraid herself.

"What's wrong, Ms. Jameson?" I asked timidly. I had startled her, and her eyes flew open. Then, she looked at me with a sorrow I had never seen in a grown-up.

"Hello… it's Ellen, correct?" she said in a whisper. "You can call me Mae. I've seen you and your sister play in the yard many times."

"Are you going on a trip?" I asked.

"I suppose you could call it that," she said with a sad smile.

"Ellen, what are you doing up?" came my mother's voice.

"I, well, I heard voices… "

"Well, everything's fine here. We're just helping Miss Mae. You need to get back to bed. You've got school tomorrow."

I took only a few steps back into the hall, just into the shadows.

"Bob, get Mae's suitcase. You'd both better leave now."

"Mae, here's your ticket. It leaves at 12:45 a.m. Nobody saw you leave, correct?"

Mae shook her head no.

"Okay, good, good. Don't draw any attention to yourself. Bob's going to drive you to the bus station. Call us when you get to Chicago. I want to know that you got there safely."

At that point, Mom realized I hadn't gone to my room.

"Ellen, come here. You didn't see Miss Mae here tonight. Do you understand? If anyone asks, and I mean anyone, you haven't seen her." She bent down to my eye level. "You know I would never ask you to lie, but, in this circumstance, you need to do what I ask, okay?"

"Okay."

Mom turned back to Mae and said, "Okay, honey, I think you're ready." She gave Mae a hug. "Bob, are you ready?"

Dad nodded as he finished putting on his coat and hat.

"Here, Mae, let me take your suitcase," he said, reaching for it. "We'd better hurry."

I watched as this strange scene played out. Miss Mae was obviously running from something, from what I wasn't sure. I didn't even know Mom or Dad had ever spoken to Miss Mae in the years we'd been living across the street from the Jamesons. We thought Crazy Mae spent most of her time in some sort of sanitarium. She didn't appear crazy to me, just sad.

I don't know why I decided at that moment to ask Miss Mae about the bird, but I did. "Hey, Miss Mae, how's Bird?"

Her face couldn't have looked any sadder. She slowly walked over to me, wrapped her arms around me, and whispered in my ear, "Bird's just fine. Bird's free." And then, with a deep sob that escaped her throat, she whimpered, "Ellen, please tell your sister I'm so very sorry."

With that, she gave me a hug, turned around, and followed my dad out the door. Mom locked the door behind them and turned off the lights. "Come here, Ellen," she said as she sat down, patting the spot next to her on the sofa. I sat next to her, feeling goosebumps on my arms and legs as I realized I was wearing my summer nightgown in November. She saw me shiver, and she put her arm around me. "You know, sometimes things happen to people through no fault of their own. When that happens, we must do what we can to help those people."

"Is that what happened to Miss Mae?" I asked.

"Yes, it did. Miss Mae was in a situation that was dangerous for her. I'm afraid her husband hasn't treated her very well."

"Like how?"

"Well, like, at times, hurting her."

"Like hitting her?"

"Yes, I'm afraid so. She was afraid and needed help. And that's why we need to keep what happened tonight to ourselves. Do you understand?"

"Yes,"

"Good girl. Now, go get some sleep," she said, kissing me on top of my head.

I crawled back into bed and pulled the covers up to my chin. What would I do if someone tried to hurt me? Would I fight back, would I run away? Would I have the courage to do something? I didn't really know.

"What's going on out there?" Jenny said in a sleepy voice.

"Nothing," I said, remembering Mom's words.

"Hey, Jenny?"

"Hmm…?" she said, barely coherent.

"Why would Miss Mae want me to tell you she was sorry?"

Silence.

"Jenny?"

"I don't know. Go to sleep," she said.

PRESENT DAY
Twenty-one

I practically fell off the porch swing realizing who Mrs. Caldwell was. She was Mae Jameson, she had to be. I jumped up in my stocking feet, tore open the front door, ran to the den, grabbed the photograph off the coffee table, and stared at the face of Mae Jameson. Older, yes, but the eyes, there was no doubt that they were the same eyes of the woman who stood in our living room over fifty years ago. My God, this is crazy. What on earth, why on earth? Mom—Mom had to have known something. We never spoke of Mae again after that night. I don't remember anyone asking any questions about her. It's like she just vanished. I never asked questions because I always followed the rules. *I've got to call Mom.* I looked at the clock; it was still early. I retrieved my phone. My hands were shaking. The phone rang, then went to voicemail. *Dammit*, I was hearing my own damn voice because I had set it up for her. "C'mon, dammit, pickup, c'mon." I dialed three more times, hoping she might eventually hear it. On the last call I left myself a message.

"Mom, it's me. Call me when you get this message. It's important! Please!"

That would have to do. Who knew how long it would take her to get around to calling me, that is if she actually checked her messages? I shouldn't complain. She did alright for her age.

"Okay, what do I do next? Let me think, let me think," I said pacing the floor.

I grabbed my laptop and phone. I refilled my wine glass and decided to relocate to the back patio. I decided I'd better grab something to eat. I didn't need to drink on an empty stomach. I made myself a decent salad, placed everything on a tray, and carried my dinner outside. Once situated in the chaise, I balanced my laptop on my lap, while holding my meal in front of me. I began searching the Internet with one hand and occasionally stopping long enough to shovel in mouthfuls of romaine. I was sure I looked like a cow chewing her cud.

I put down my fork and tried to focus on where I needed to look for answers first. "I know the year was 1963."

I could remember thinking that my whole world was falling apart during the fall and winter of 1963. That was the year Jack was so sick, Jenny had been found in the closet traumatized by something or someone, Kennedy had been assassinated along with his killer, Charlie died, and, yes, somewhere in between all that, there was the Jamesons. It was a time period I chose to keep to myself and not dwell on. I guess because it always made me sad to think about those days. So, I didn't—not much anyway. I have always been good at compartmentalizing. Why bring up bad memories? They only serve to expose old wounds. It wasn't in my best interest to dwell on the unpleasant past. But now I was being challenged to face them head on.

I sat up and began my search. First, I would start with my hometown newspapers, *The Courier,* which my father worked for, and its competitor, *The News Gazette.* I typed in the following keywords into the computer: Champaign, Illinois; *The Courier*; *The News Gazette*; Jamesons; murder; suicide; 1963. I hit Enter. Like magic, a series of results appeared. I stared at the screen as the list, highlighted in blue, became a pathway for answers.

"Here we go," I said while shaking my head at the information that lay before me.

I clicked on the first result which was a newspaper article in *The Courier* from November 8, 1963: "Was It a Murder/Suicide or Just Plain Murder?"

> On the afternoon of Wednesday, November 6, the bodies of thirty-eight-year-old Henry Jameson, and his seventy-seven-year-old father, Luther Jameson, were discovered in their home located on Bakers Court in Champaign. Henry Jameson's death was

apparently the result of a gunshot wound to the head, however, Luther Jameson succumbed to head injuries from a fall, according to police. The coroner has concluded that the decomposition of the bodies appears to show that death occurred at least two or three days prior. The deaths are still under investigation, and they have not ruled out the possibility of either murder/suicide or a double homicide. Henry Jameson leaves behind a wife, Mae (Billings) Jameson, previously of Savoy, who is currently being sought for questioning. Anyone with any information regarding the deaths of Henry and/or Luther Jameson, or the whereabouts of Mae Jameson, are asked to contact the Champaign County Police Department.

I was numb. Madeline, I mean Mae, had possibly been a murderer or was wanted in connection to the murder of her husband and father-in-law. Mae had been from Savoy. Reverend Hollister had heard her correctly that day they were together sorting the children's Bibles. Her father probably had been a pastor in Savoy at one time. That would be relatively easy to find information on. Savoy was a small town, even today. Somehow, I knew that this story, Mae's story, happened after she married Henry Jameson. I tried to remember the death of the Jamesons. Maybe there was just so much going on during that time period that I tuned it out. I do remember that there was a trauma across the street, and that they had died, but not a lot of specifics. Maybe a vague reference here and there by Mom and Dad in passing, or neighbors in the cul-de-sac. I can remember some of the kids in the neighborhood joking about how Crazy Mae whacked her husband, but it was always just a joke. I laughed along with them, never once mentioning a word to anyone about the night and Mom and Dad helped Mae. And Jenny, she *never* laughed about it. Ordinarily, Jenny would have been right in there with them, laughing about Crazy Mae. But Jenny had changed. Jenny would never again be the Jenny I remembered. The days of riding bikes on the playground were gone. Oh, she would still come to challenge authority, but it's as if her spirit had been broken that year. I thought about the night I saw Mae in our living room. My parents wouldn't have protected a murderer, would they have? The Jamesons were strange men, at least Henry was. And then, the years passed, the memories faded, and our family moved away. I wasted little time looking back on those days.

I spent the next hour looking at the other information that I learned from the search. There was another article in *The News Gazette* that basically covered the same ground as *The Courier*. I found each man's obituary. Henry was born and raised in Philo, Illinois. He had served in the Korean War, married Mae Billings in 1953, and was an employee of Sealtest Dairy at the time of his death. His father, Luther Jameson, had been a dairy farmer who had owned and worked eighty acres of farmland in Philo before selling the farm in the late 1950s. After his father gave up the farm, Henry Jameson had moved Luther in with him and his wife. The rest of the obituary just gave the funeral arrangements for each of them.

I realized I was now sitting in the dark. The mosquitos were beginning to find me appealing. I got up and stretched. It was time to move indoors. I looked at my watch, it was after 9:30 p.m. I still hadn't heard from Mom. I'd try and call her again in the morning. I brought everything inside, dumping my dishes in the sink and all other items on the coffee table in the den. I hadn't let Lilly come out with me, so I knew I owed her a potty break. But me first. I quickly made a pit stop, found some bug spray in my suitcase, and generously applied it to my bare legs and arms. I found Lilly's leash and attached it to her collar, grabbed my phone, and headed out the front door. She was taking her time, and I let her. I was in no real hurry to do anything. I was trying to process everything I had just learned and figure out what I truly remembered. I realized I had Hunter McGaffey and his daughters coming tomorrow. *Oh, Christ!* I thought. *What will I tell him? Nothing. I will tell him nothing right now. I'm not ready to share any of this with anyone.* I would hold off telling him anything until I understood more myself. I then realized I had invited them to stay for lunch. I hoped I had something in the fridge to feed them. If not, I'd be making an early morning run to the grocery.

"C'mon, Lilly, hurry up, I'm getting eaten alive." Even the bug spray didn't prove to be much of a repellant for these southern bloodsuckers. "Okay, I'm giving you thirty more seconds, and then we're done here," I threatened her. She must have understood because she immediately took care of business.

"Good girl. Let's go."

My phone began to ring. It was Mom.

"Hey, there, thanks for calling me back," I said.

"I hope it's not too late to call. I was playing bridge, and you know how long it takes Laverne to bid. I thought we'd still be there for breakfast." Mom and her best friend Laverne had moved into a senior living facility a couple of years ago. Laverne had lost her husband the same year we'd lost Dad. The two friends decided they'd make the move together, choosing their own separate apartments, but in the same facility. They were ready to leave the upkeep of owning a home behind. Now they seemed to enjoy the comforts of being close to one another, but that also included them fussing about each other like an old married couple. Whatever, as long as they're happy and enjoying their twilight years.

"Uh, Mom, I need you to help me with something. Something that happened back in Illinois."

There was silence on the other end.

"Mom, are you there?"

"Yes, what do you need help with?"

I took a deep breath, let it out slowly, and began…

The words tumbled out so fast I know I sounded like a lunatic. I tried to explain everything that had happened thus far and how I'd come to realize Mrs. Caldwell was really Mae Jameson.

"Well, that's quite a story," was her only reply.

"Mom, seriously? That's it? That's all you got?"

"Well, I don't know, Ellen. That was so long ago. You say that this woman left you her house and that this woman is really Mae Jameson?"

"*Was* Mae Jameson, Mom. *Was!*"

"Hm. Well, isn't that something?"

I was about to explode. "Mom, look, I need you to think back. Do you remember the night you and Dad helped Mae?"

"Golly, that was so long ago. Those days were such a blur because I was so tired all the time. Between Jack and Charlie, I walked around without much sleep. But let me think. I vaguely remember it was late at night. I think your dad drove her to the bus stop."

"Do you remember that I got up? Do you remember that?"

"Oh, Ellen, I really don't remember the details. I'm sorry."

"Okay, I understand. Maybe you just need some time to think about it. I know it's been years."

"Yes, it has."

I wasn't ready to let it go yet.

"Well, let me ask you this," I persisted. "Do you remember how you even came to help her? I mean, you really didn't know her well, right? I mean, she didn't come over to the house or anything before that night. Did she? How did you even know she was in trouble?"

"No, we didn't really know her. I would see her from time to time from across the street, and I'd wave. She always seemed quite sad," she said.

"Okay, but still, how did you know to help her?"

"Um, gosh, I don't, oh wait, wait. It was Dorothy. Dorothy asked us to help her," she said.

"Dorothy?"

"Yes, Dorothy. I think that was her name. She lived next door to the Jamesons."

"Wait! Was her last name Gallagher? Was she Dorothy Gallagher, Mom?" My brain began to fire on all cylinders.

"Yes, that's it! Dorothy Gallagher."

"Dorothy Gallagher. Oh, my God!" And, suddenly, another piece of the puzzle had fallen into place. Evelyn Murray was Dorothy Gallagher.

1963

Twenty-two

"You wanna ride bikes?" I asked Jenny as we changed from our school clothes into our play clothes. That was the rule. Before snacks, watching TV, or anything else we might have on our agenda after school, we had to change our clothes. Mom said we couldn't afford to buy new clothes for school, and she absolutely would not let us go to school with clothes that had holes or grass stains.

"No," Jenny said.

"Oh, c'mon. I don't want to stay inside. It's still nice out."

"No."

"Oh, alright, I'll see if Brenda Jean can play," I said, hoping that it might stir her a bit.

It didn't. Nothing. No response.

She hadn't wanted to do anything at all lately. She'd just stay in her room, laying on her bed. *God, I wish she'd snap out of it.* It had been almost a week since "that night" and you'd think she'd be over it. The last time I saw her excited had been on Halloween, just a few days before we found her lying in the closet. Mom let us stay out a bit later to trick-or-treat. When it was time to go home, Jenny and I ran back as fast as we could, eager to dump our sagging pillowcases and take inventory of our bounty. When we dashed through the front door, we immediately sat down on the living room rug and began systematically categorizing our sweet stash into piles. We laughed as we sifted through our treasures, talking nonstop about the fun we'd had. It was a great night. That seemed so long ago now. I looked at her for a full thirty seconds. Still, no response.

"Fine," I said as I turned my back to her and put on my jacket. I stopped just short of the door and glanced back. Nothing. She was pretending to read a book, but I knew Jenny, she didn't read books. I did.

"I know you're not reading that!"

"No, you don't."

"Yes, I do. So, what's it about?"

"Read it yourself if you want to know."

"I've already read it, so I already know. You don't know because you're not really reading it," I pressed on, hoping to get a reaction. Still nothing. I stuck my tongue out at her and left.

The day was still relatively warm for early November. There was still enough daylight left to spend a good amount of time outside before coming home for supper. I grabbed my bike and pedaled onto the circle. Out of the corner of my eye, I caught something small, an animal of some sort sitting at the end of Miss Gallagher's driveway. I didn't want to scare whatever it was, so I circled the cul-de-sac and came to a stop in front of the Jamesons' yard, just far enough away so as not to spook it. I got off my bike ever so slowly, gently pushed down the kickstand with my foot, and walked toward the driveway until I was able to make out what it was. *Aww*, it was a kitten, a little gray ball of fur so tiny it looked like it could practically fit in the palm of my hand. I gently approached. It didn't move. It looked so scared. Was it hurt? I ever so gently sat down next to it.

"Hey, there, little fella, where's your mama?" I asked as I reached out to pet the little guy. I couldn't tell whether it was a girl or boy, but it looked like a boy to me. No logic, just intuition. It gave out a single *meow* but made no attempt to move.

"What's wrong, little fella? Are you sick or hurt?" I asked as I continued to stroke his fur. I must have sat with that cat for several minutes, until the gravel from the driveway made permanent indentations on my thighs.

"C'mon, let's move you off the driveway," I whispered in its ear.

I gently picked up the kitten, hoping I wasn't hurting the animal. I moved it to Miss Gallagher's front yard. I sat next to him. He didn't fight me. In fact, once deposited on the grass, it literally stretched its little legs, arched its back, and crawled into my lap. I flinched as his sharp little claws made contact with my flesh under my thin trousers. I braced myself as he kneaded into my skin, finding a more comfortable position.

"Mom will never let me keep you," I said in a whisper. Jenny was terrified of cats, ever since a rabid cat chased her up the swing set the year before. I smiled just thinking about it when a voice screeched from behind me.

"What the hell are you doing?"

I jumped, the kitten leapt off my lap and dashed under Ms. Gallagher's car that had been parked a few feet up the driveway.

"Oh no! You scared him!" I yelled running towards the car.

"Get on out of here!" she screamed from her front porch.

I stood my ground. Miss Gallagher's face was full of rage, but I didn't care. I was a protector of all animals, well, except for that snake my brother tried to throw at me.

"It's just a little kitten, Miss Gallagher. You've scared it, now it ran under your car."

"I don't care!"

"No, I want to make sure it's okay," I said, kneeling under her car, trying to see where it had gone.

"Get away from my car!" she demanded.

I ignored her. I went around the other side of the car, putting distance between Miss Gallagher and me. The kitten was hiding behind the right front tire. I reached under and grabbed the cat, cradling it to my chest.

I walked to the back of the car, showing Miss Gallagher the kitten.

"See? It's just a kitten."

"Get it out of here, and you too!" she hissed.

At the sound of her voice, the kitten jumped from my arms, dashed around the side of the Jamesons' house, and made a beeline for the railroad tracks. Tears formed, stinging my eyes. I was heartsick. I knew I wouldn't see that kitten again. I hated that woman at that moment. Miss Gallagher was standing on her front porch, still holding her screen door open with one hand, glaring at me, and waiting for me to leave.

I don't know why, or where it came from, but it was as if Jenny was behind me, pushing me forward. I stopped short of her front porch, held my head high, looked her right in the eye, and said in a voice I didn't even recognize, "You know, you're an awful person." Tears fell down my cheeks. "You're nothing but an old witch."

I watched as her face completely transformed. Hurt replaced rage.

With satisfaction, I turned around, retrieved my bike from the Jamesons' yard, and went home.

Twenty-three

I woke to a vibration in my right hand. It was my phone. I must have mistakenly put it on silent sometime later in the evening because it wasn't on silent when Mom called me back last night. I sat up and blinked, trying to get the sleep out of my eyes. It was Dan. We seemed to be establishing this morning ritual.

"Good morning," I said, trying to clear my head and throat.

"Well, hey sleepy head, you still in bed?"

"Technically, I'm not in bed. I'm on the couch. What time is it anyway?" I asked.

"Well, let's see. It's almost 10:00 a.m. our time. Brunswick's in the Eastern time zone, same as

206

Louisville, I think."

"Oh shit, wow! How did I sleep that long? Listen, Dan, can I call you back? I've got to get in the shower and head out to the store. I've invited Hunter McGaffey and his girls over this afternoon. The girls want to visit their aunt's gravesite here on the property, and I invited them to stay for lunch afterward. I don't have a damn thing to feed them."

"Sure, you get going."

I suddenly felt like a heel. *Jesus, Ellen*, I thought. *How can you be so dismissive, so insensitive? It's not all about you for Christ's sake. Get your priorities straight!*

"Hey, I'm sorry, really. How ya holdin' up?" I asked.

"I'm doing okay."

"Listen, I'm sorry. I don't want to sound uncaring. I know you're going through this alone, and I should be there. I'm afraid I've became consumed with trying to find some answers, and it's taking over my thinking. I promise I will be home sometime next week; I promise. No matter what, okay? I'm almost there in finding out what this is all about. I can feel it. And you know what? If I don't figure it out, it doesn't matter, I'm coming home anyway. You know that you are the most important thing in my life. You know that, don't you?"

"I know."

"I promise I'll give you a call later this afternoon and fill you in on what I've learned so far."

"From the sounds of it, you might have some viable leads then?"

"Well, you're not going to believe this, but one of my most promising leads was my own mother! She actually filled me in on a few pieces of the puzzle."

"Oh really, your mom? Well, now I'm intrigued," he said.

I laughed. "I know, right! Who'd have thought *she* held a few of the answers? Anyway, I'll give you a call later this afternoon and fill you in. I love you."

"I love you, too. Bye." As quick as the conversation began, it ended. Suddenly, I felt exhausted. I think I dreamed most of last night, but, for the life of me, I couldn't remember about what. I felt as tired at that moment as I had last night. My conversation with Mom left me drained. The last thing I remember after getting off the phone with her was collapsing on the couch. I realized I was still in that exact position, wearing the same clothes.

Get up. I willed myself off the couch.

I slowly moved my sore, stiff limbs, turned the ringer back on, and got up to find an outlet. I realized I had slept with the phone by my side all night and it was now running on ten percent of its power. I then tended to Lilly and made a dash for the shower. I was now fully awake, feeling revitalized. Within a half hour, I was wearing my favorite pink sleeveless summer dress—well, actually, one of the two dresses I brought with me, and my white sneakers. I thought about sandals but realized if the gravesite was a bit of a walk from the house, I wasn't going to traipse around in sandals. I managed a little makeup, put a comb through my hair, and headed out the door.

Once in the car, I quickly Googled the closest grocery store, found an address, and put it in my GPS. I was ready to face the day. Another warm one in Georgia, but not nearly as humid as it had been the last few days. I shut off the air conditioning and rolled down the window. I turned on the radio and fiddled with it until I heard Queen's "Radio Ga Ga." That made me happy. I traveled down the highway, feeling freer than I'd felt in a long time, with my elbow resting on the door of the open window, my fingers tapping to Queen. I wouldn't have minded doing this for the rest of the day, just driving down a two-lane highway, listening to music, enjoying the Georgia summer. However, the grocery story appeared sooner than I would have liked, so my euphoria would have to be put on hold.

I didn't realize just how warm the day was already until the blast of cool air hit me as I entered the store. *Brrrrr*…suddenly my sleeveless dress didn't provide much protection from the Arctic air that just went up my skirt. *Jeez. Okay, let's make this quick.*

I grabbed a cart and headed past the cashiers, trying to get the lay of the land. I saw a sign for the deli and headed in that direction. I found the cheese shop first and picked up a nice Brie, a wedge of Pennsylvania Dutch blue cheese along with some wafer-like crackers. Next, I selected some spring-mix greens for a salad, a few Honeycrisp apples—my very favorite—and a bag of walnuts. I picked up a rotisserie chicken that smelled so heavenly I almost opened the bag and tore into it right there on the spot. I realized I hadn't even stopped to have breakfast this morning. I swung by the bakery and picked up a lovely angel food cake and a blueberry muffin for the drive home, and then swung back around once more to the produce, selecting a pack of fresh strawberries.

"Oh, look, daisies, my favorites," I said to no one in particular, as I sailed past a display of fresh-cut flowers. I stopped and picked out the prettiest bunch I could find and placed them up front—the premium seat in the cart, next to my purse. I was almost to the checkout line when I realized I needed whipped cream for the strawberries. *I'll put together some semblance of strawberry shortcake for dessert.* I spun the cart around and had a head-on collision with the cart behind me.

"Whoa! Slow her down," said an extremely familiar voice.

"Oh, my gosh!" My eyes widened as I recognized Judy Cameron from the law office standing behind the cart I had just slammed into. "Hi there! I am so sorry! I wasn't watching where I was going. Are you okay?"

"I'm just fine, sweetie," she said with a laugh. She gazed into my cart and asked, "Is all that for you?"

"Oh no," I laughed. I told her about my plans for that afternoon.

"Oh, my. You're now entertaining the handsome Dr. McGaffey? A gravesite picnic, how romantic," she said with a mischievous twinkle in her eye.

"Oh Lord no! Don't go getting any ideas, lady. First of all, I'm happily married. Second of all, he's a wee bit younger than me. Third, his teenage girls are coming with him, and fourth, a graveyard rendezvous isn't exactly my style."

"Well, sweetie, I haven't heard one thing in your testimony that leads me to believe that any of that makes any difference whatsoever," she said with a grin.

"Well, you are wrong," I said with a smile. "So, what are you doing out this way?"

"Oh, this is one of my favorite haunts. I try to get here every couple of weeks. Their deli and cheese shop are the bomb. But I can see from your cart you've already discovered that."

"Yes, yes I have. It's wonderful. I think I put on a few pounds just browsing," I laughed. "Uh, listen, Judy," I said changing gears, "not to change the subject, but I'm, um, going to call Jimmy on Monday. I've found some information that I'd like to share with him. Do you know if he'll be in?"

"Honey, that man's always in."

"Oh, good. It's real important that I see him before I go. Do you think he'll find some time for me?"

"Go? Why, sweetie, you just got here! I was so hoping to get to know you better, sugar."

"That's so sweet. I feel like we've known each other all our lives." Funny how some people just make you feel that way. "Besides, I didn't say I wouldn't come back. But my family, especially my husband, needs me right now, and I think I might actually be close to finding out what brought me here in the first place."

"Do I have to remind you that a multi-million-dollar estate brought you here?" she said with a wry smile.

"No, I'm well aware of that," I said, smiling back. "But the why, that's what I need to see him about."

"Listen, I'll let him know when I get in on Monday. We've got a new girl working the phones temporarily, but I'll make sure she knows you'll be calling, okay?"

"Oh, Judy, that would be great, thank you."

"Are you really okay? Is everything alright?" she asked, genuinely concerned.

"To be perfectly honest, I don't really know. Maybe," I said with a shrug.

"Well, if there's anything I can do, you just let me know," she said, giving my arm a squeeze.

"You're a doll, thank you. I'd better get going. Don't want to be late for my picnic in the graveyard," I said with a wink.

"You have fun now. Maybe I'll catch you on Monday when you come in to see Jimmy," she said.

"I'll look for you. Take care," I said as I hugged her goodbye.

"You too, sugar."

I hurried off before I started to cry. How silly. I've seen the women twice and I feel like I'm leaving my best friend.

Get a hold of yourself, Ellen, I thought. *Concentrate on the task at hand, and that would be finding the damned whipped cream and getting out of this icebox they call a grocery store.*

I made it back in time to not only put everything away, but arrange the cheese, fruit, and chicken on platters. All I would have to do is pull everything out of the refrigerator. I set the table and was glad that I spotted the daisies before leaving the store. I found a small glass tumbler under the sink, filled it with water, and added the flowers to the table. It was the best I could do with the time I had. I glanced at the clock and saw that it was a few minutes after 1:00 p.m. They were obviously running a little behind. *No problem.* I was nervous. Well, who wouldn't be? This was their family's house. The buzzer sounded, my heart skipped a beat, I took a moment to compose myself, then I made my way to the foyer.

"Hello?"

"Hi, Ellen, it's Hunter and the girls."

"Great! Come on through," I said as I punched in the code to allow them to enter. Lilly and I waited on the front steps to greet them. I know I must have thought this a hundred times before, but it still all seemed so strange.

"Here we go again, Lilly. Standing here, feeling like fools, imposters. No, I know you feel no guilt whatsoever. You have no shame," I said as she stood there, tongue hanging out, looking as laid back as a dog could get.

I wondered how many times the Caldwells stood in this exact spot, greeting their guests or saying goodbye.

Hunter pulled up in the white convertible. Neither he nor the girls looked like they had one hair out of place. If it had been me riding in that car, I would be looking like I had just stuck my finger in a light socket. Lilly and I made our way down the steps to greet them.

"Hello, I'm Ellen," I said with a smile to the pretty blond who emerged from the front seat. She wasn't just pretty; she was stunningly beautiful. It was obvious she was the older of the two.

"Hi, I'm Claire," she said taking my outstretched hand in her French manicured one.

"And you are?" I asked, turning to the pretty petite brunette, whose dimples were as adorable as her wide smile. She was about to shake my hand when Lilly decided she would rather be introduced first as she jumped upon her.

"I'm Maggie," she laughed as she grabbed Lilly around the waist and gave her a bear hug. This kid stole my heart. She was an animal lover.

"Oh gosh! Sorry! Lilly, down! She has no manners. It wasn't from lack of trying, really, I have tried," I said laughing.

"It's okay, I love dogs. Hi, girl, it's nice to meet you, too," Maggie said with a smile.

"Well, as I told your dad the first time we met, you get a free lint roller with every visit. Please, come in," I said, leading them up the steps and through the front door. Lilly bounded up the stairs, ahead of all of us, happy that there were new people to play with. The girls stopped in the foyer and did a 360. I knew they were taking it all in, all the memories. I stayed quiet, letting them have their time.

Claire spoke first. "It's funny, the house still feels like Aunt Del."

"I know. I miss her," said Maggie. "Claire, do you remember the Christmas we decided we'd see how many candy canes we could throw into the tree from the top of the stairs?" she asked, pointing to the landing above.

"Yeah, I believe I won with fifteen."

"No, you didn't, I think that would be me," she chuckled.

"I remember we almost hit Uncle Anderson in the head with a flying candy cane when he walked into the foyer," laughed Claire.

"Oh yeah, he turned around without missing a beat; he picked it up and sailed it right back up at us. Aunt Del just laughed," Maggie said while keeping her gaze on the staircase. "I loved Christmases here. They were so magical."

"They were, girls. Aunt Del and Uncle Anderson made them special."

Oh, dear God! I thought to myself. Well, if I wasn't feeling like a total idiot before, I truly was now. Was that Hunter McGaffey's plan all along? To get the girls here, start reminiscing about Christmases past, make me feel like nothing short of Ebenezer Scrooge, then swoop in for the kill? I really didn't think that was the case, but if it was, he didn't have to go to that much trouble. I had already made up my mind that unless I found some reason for not giving the property back to the family, that's exactly what I intended to do.

"Well," Hunter said, clearing his throat, and clapping his surgeon's hands together, "I'm sure Ellen has more important things to do today than listen to us reminisce."

"No, please, I want to know more about your aunt and uncle. From what I've heard, they were extraordinary people," I said sincerely.

"Oh, that's right. You didn't know them, did you?" Claire asked with just a hint of arrogance. I looked at her and all I could see was Jenny's face. *Oh Claire*, I thought to myself, *I've dealt with someone far more challenging than you, my dear.*

"Well, I'm certainly beginning to know them," I said as I led them out of the foyer, into the den, and toward the French doors. "Shall we?" I said, indicating it was time to visit Aunt Madeline and Uncle Anderson. "Claire, would you like to lead us?"

"Sure," she said, stepping around me and exiting to the patio.

"Can we bring Lilly?" Maggie asked.

"Oh, absolutely!" I said, handing Maggie the leash.

"C'mon, girl," she said as she led Lilly out the door.

Hunter was wearing a small smile on his face. I wasn't sure what that meant, but to be perfectly honest, it didn't really matter. These were good people. Maybe a bit spoiled, but who was I to judge? They were a nice family, that much was clear, and they had loved their aunt and uncle. Hunter and I brought up the rear. I hadn't investigated this part of the property before. To be perfectly honest, the property was so vast that I was actually afraid I might get lost.

There were stone steps that descended from the patio. When I reached the bottom, I was absolutely speechless. From the patio, you could only see the rolling hills and the river in the distance—which itself was a beautiful view. But this, this was altogether something else. And if you didn't know the property, you had no idea the wonder that awaited you at the end of those steps. I felt like Dorothy from the *Wizard of Oz* after the tornado, as she opened the door from her house into Munchkinland. I'd never seen so many vibrant perennials and flowering shrubs. There were purples, pinks, reds, yellows, and so many shades of green I couldn't focus my eyes. "My God! I didn't even know this existed!" I said in total astonishment.

"Aunt Del did love her flowers," he said.

"Well, that's an understatement," I said staring at him and then back at the glory around me. "Who keeps up with all of this?"

He laughed at my apparent astonishment. "Well, that would be you from here on out. But she had a service that would come once a month to take care of the grounds. I'm assuming that's still ongoing, but you might want to check on that."

"Oh, that's right, I was told that she secured a property manager who was taking care of the house and grounds until, well, whenever...," I let the sentence trail off.

The girls were already way ahead. They had turned right and disappeared through a thick grove of trees, staying on a stone path. I stopped gawking and started walking again. It was apparent that we were heading up a hilly area. I wasn't short of breath, but I was glad I decided to wear my tennis shoes. The stone trail ended, and we found ourselves on a foot path. We walked for several minutes, making our way up a steady incline, through a densely wooded area. We entered a large clearing. The area was quartered off with what looked like wood fencing, almost something you'd see out of the Civil War era, something out of Gettysburg. Inside the fence was a massive oak tree. And just to the right of the tree were two beautifully matching headstones made of steel gray granite. The headstones were positioned in such a way that the sun would set directly behind them to the west, showcasing the spectacular view of the river to the south. A stone bench had been placed under the tree, allowing for shade and comfort to whomever came to visit. "It's glorious," was all I could say. I walked over, took the leash from Maggie, and guided Lilly back to the opening of the fence.

I waited there with Lilly to give the family some privacy. I watched as Hunter stood with his girls, heads together, bowed. I hadn't noticed it before, but Maggie was holding pink peonies that she must have plucked from the garden on the way up. I watched as she placed them on her aunt's grave.

I didn't approach the grave that day. I knew I would most assuredly come back and say goodbye. A large black bird flew in from the north, landing just a few feet from Lilly and me on the fence. Lilly didn't move. I didn't move. The bird didn't make a sound. We just stood there facing one another, staring straight into each other's eyes. Finally, it lifted its clawed foot and shook it, then lifted the other and did the same. It moved down the fence, inch by inch. It stopped no less than a foot from where I stood. I watched it. It watched me. I raised my head and gave it a nod, "Hey, Bird," I simply said. It dipped its head up and down as if to acknowledge my salutation. It spread its wings and flew away.

As we left the gravesite and made our way back to the house for lunch, I told Hunter that I hadn't learned much from my visit with Evelyn. That she wasn't very responsive. I wasn't exactly lying, but I really didn't know enough yet to tell him, or if I'd ever tell him anything. I didn't feel guilty. It was my story to tell, once I knew what that story was.

I put lunch on the table as soon as we got back. We

ate and laughed as the girls told stories of being allowed to rummage through their great aunt's closet, trying on her hats, dresses, and jewelry. They would unwrap her silk scarves, lay them on the floor, and use them as a runway, modeling for her. Their aunt would throw back her head and laugh, then clap her hands and say, "Let's see more."

I felt I knew Madeline a little bit more through the eyes of her great nieces. Claire even seemed to warm up a bit. I understood her bitterness. I would feel the same.

It was late afternoon when Lilly and I said goodbye to the McGaffeys. I assured Hunter I would be in touch in the not-so-distant future. Maggie gave Lilly a hug, then turned and hugged me. I don't know why it surprised me, but it did.

"It was so nice meeting you, Maggie."

"It was nice meeting you, too. Goodbye, Lilly," she said as she scrambled into the back seat.

"Goodbye, Claire, it was a pleasure," I said.

"It was nice meeting you, Ellen. Thanks for having us."

I just smiled. I didn't know what else to say.

Lilly and I stayed on the porch and waved to them as they pulled out.

I went in to call Dan. I needed a touch of home about now.

Twenty-four

I spent the rest of the weekend exploring the house and gardens. On Sunday, I wandered into the judge's study and leafed through the remnants of his desk. I felt like an intruder, but it didn't stop me from searching. There was a saved letter from an old friend from Pittsburgh, obviously another judge or possibly an attorney from its tone, the contents being relevant only to the judge. There were notes about pending court cases on a stenographer's pad in what I could only assume was the judge's handwriting, an old-fashioned cartridge pen, an ink blot along with the judge's signature stamp. Nothing useful to my cause. I left the judge's study and entered Madeline's room. I stood there for a full minute. Maybe I was waiting for her ghost or some apparition. Nothing appeared. The only startling thing that happened was when Lilly nudged my hand with her cold, wet nose. I looked around. I had already searched the contents of the drawers and hope chest. I hadn't really explored her closet, remembering the McGaffey girls as they regaled us with their stories at lunch. I walked into the closet. It was organized, well, tidy would best describe it. It was a definite reflection of who it had served. There were at least twenty boxes of shoes located on the top shelf that were stacked above hanging garment bags housing suits and coats. On the other side of the closet were her dresses, blouses, and slacks, hanging neatly on fabric hangers and coordinated by color. Purses and hat boxes were neatly stacked above those clothes. There was a faint scent of lilac in the air. In the corner was a valet, which was home to a large, oversized jewelry box.

"Oh, boy, I have a feeling this is going to take a while."

I spent the next two hours going through every box and all the pockets of each garment in the place. It was as if I had stepped into a vintage consignment shop. Almost everything in that closet screamed 1960s and seventies. There were pillbox hats, silk scarves, gloves, and shoes in every color you could imagine. She was a size six, both shoe size and dress size. No hope of me borrowing anything in this closet, except for maybe the jewelry. There were loads of rhinestone pins to be worn on the lapel of a coat or a suit. Numerous pairs of clip-on earrings, from pearl drops to sparkling rhinestones, matching bracelets, and several strands of pearls. I could just picture Maggie and Claire twirling in all this finery, modeling for Madeline. But even after enjoying the surprises that came with every beautiful item revealed, there was nothing in that closet that led me to any answers. I was depressed. I needed air.

I went downstairs and found Lilly's leash, plugged my earphones in, and listened to my favorite playlist as I walked around the grounds with Lilly. I was resigned to the fact that this would most likely be my last full day here. I wanted to remember everything. Tomorrow, I would see Jimmy Carmichael and give him permission to transfer the estate to the McGaffey family. I had discovered the identity of both women. That was something. Maybe, in time, I would discover the rest. I was hoping that the attorney might be able to help me now that I had found Madeline's true identity, but I wasn't banking on it. I just needed to put this to rest.

I didn't sleep well. I got up early and began packing my things. Regardless of what today might bring, I would be leaving. I stood at the kitchen sink, eating a bowl of cornflakes with strawberries. I looked at the clock. It was too early for the attorney's office to be open. I poured a second cup of coffee and took it out to the patio. It was hard to believe I'd arrived here less than a week ago. I felt different. I couldn't explain it. I looked to the river. *This is what heaven should look and feel like. I must have my head examined for giving all this up.* But I knew in my heart I could never keep it. I finished my coffee, checked the time on my phone, and called the lawyer.

Jimmy could see me at 10:30 a.m. No problem. I could be there. I hopped in the shower, dressing quickly in a pair of navy capris and a white sleeveless blouse, and, of course, my white Keds. I needed to be comfortable. I tidied up the den and kitchen. I left my suitcase and pillow by the front door, along with the cooler I had brought and a box of food items I could take back home. I'd clean out the fridge when I got back and pitch anything perishable.

"And, no, Lilly, I won't forget you," I said, patting her head as I left.

I arrived at the attorneys' office with five minutes to spare. The new receptionist flashed a perfectly white smile and asked me to have a seat. I didn't see Judy, but I could hear that southern drawl of hers wafting down the hallway. She apparently was on the phone. Jimmy came out to greet me. He looked like he was wearing the exact same outfit he had been wearing the day I met him. The only difference was he was sporting a partial goatee of white powdered sugar, apparently from the half-eaten powdered doughnut in his left hand.

"Ellen, can I get you anything? Coffee, a doughnut? Don't tell my wife, I keep a box of these things in the break room."

"Coffee might be nice," I said, following him down the hall.

Judy's door was slightly ajar, and I only caught a small glimpse of her and waved.

"Please, have a seat. How do you take your coffee?"

"Just black, thanks." There was something reassuring about Jimmy Carmichael. The fact that he fetched coffee for his clients and didn't expect anyone else to do it for him impressed me. He came back, holding a steaming cup. "Here you go," he said, wiping his mouth with the napkin. "Now, Ellen, what can I do for you?"

I told him everything. I told him about my hunt for the truth. I told him about my failure to find out anything more than the identities of the two women from my past, Dorothy Gallagher and Mae Jameson. I told him my wishes for the estate. I told him it was time for me to go home.

He listened intently, not once interrupting. As soon as I was finished, he got up, opened his filing cabinet, and extracted a folder. Without speaking, he sat back down at his desk and opened the folder containing what looked to be a sealed manila envelope.

"Let me begin by saying that I wished I'd been able to give you this when you first arrived. It would probably have saved you a lot of time and sleepless nights. However, I was under strict instructions by Mrs. Caldwell to only give it you. And only under the condition that you, and you alone, gave me the name Mae Jameson. I was never told by Mrs. Caldwell who Mae Jameson was. Of course, I had my suspicions, but, due to attorney-client privilege, everything was kept confidential, and I only asked questions that were absolutely necessary. In the event you had not discovered the name, I was to destroy the envelope and its contents exactly three years after the date of her death. I don't know why. I have never seen the contents of this envelope. It is yours now. Do with it what you want."

I was stunned. I never expected this. My hands were

shaking so much that I had to put my coffee cup down before I spilled it in in my lap.

He handed me the envelope. "Would you like some privacy?" he asked.

I was overwhelmed with emotion and scared to death. I sat there clutching the envelope, afraid to open it, afraid to not open it.

"No," I finally said. "No, that's alright. I'll take it with me."

I stood up to leave. I couldn't make my legs move. I sat back down again. "I'm sorry, just give me a minute," I said.

"Of course, can I get you a glass of water?"

"No, no I'm fine. I'll be fine. Listen," I said as soon as I was able to get my bearings, "can I contact you later about the estate? I really can't think right now."

"Of course. I think you have my card, but here's another just in case," he said, handing me his business card from the holder on his desk.

"Yes, thank you. I'll be in touch," I said as I found my legs and got up to leave.

Jimmy gently placed his hand under my elbow and helped guide me to the door. I placed my hand on his arm in gratitude.

"Thank you for your help."

"You bet. You take care of yourself. Call me

whenever you're ready."

"I will," I said.

I barely remember driving back to the Caldwells. I didn't even say goodbye to Judy on my way out. I couldn't have found my voice even if I had wanted too. I entered the house and stood in the middle of the foyer. Lilly greeted me. I held the envelope. I knew what I needed to do.

It was almost 1:00 p.m. by the time Lilly and I entered the gravesite. I hadn't approached either headstone on Saturday, but today, I stood in front of both, reading each inscription. *In loving memory, Anderson B. Caldwell. Loving husband, man of justice. Born: January 18, 1920. Died: March 7, 2007.* And the other. *In loving memory, Madeline Caldwell. Loving wife, forever soaring the heavens on gossamer wings. Died: July 17, 2018.* There was no birthdate.

I walked over to the bench, giving Lilly the sign to lie down. I sat. My heart was beating. I swallowed. *Open it*, I heard my sister say. With shaking hands, I opened it.

July 10, 2018

Dear Ellen,

If you are reading this, then you are exactly the kind of girl I thought you were. Mostly quiet in disposition, but tenacious in spirit and fortitude. And I hope you are forgiving. Only then will I be able to truly forgive myself. You are stronger than me. If I had been stronger, I would have confronted the truth long before this. But, I did not. I know that I am in no way deserving of your forgiveness, nor do I deserve Jenny's, but I can only hope. There hasn't been a single day that has gone by since that horrible day that I haven't thought about Jenny. I will carry that with me to my grave. If Jenny were still alive, if she had managed to survive all this, I would be addressing her right now. So, you are her sister, the only other person in her life who shared that unique childhood bond, and you deserve to know the truth. I have kept up with you girls since the day I fled Champaign. That day in Savannah, the one where you were on holiday with your girlfriend, do you remember the photograph taken in Forsyth Park and the gentleman who took that photograph? I'd been paying this gentleman for several years to keep me informed of you and your sister's lives and whereabouts. I've known about Jenny's lifelong struggles. I learned of her suicide. It broke my heart. I remembered back to that night in your living room, when I saw you standing there so small in your nightgown, and you asked me what was wrong. I don't even know if telling you now will hurt you more than it will help. It might, though, help you understand some of your sister's pain. I know no other way to show you the depth of my sorrow for the past than to leave you my most precious possession, my home. I hope you will accept it on behalf of your sister. So, Ellen, here is what happened on that day.

It was November 4, 1963. I knew as soon as he got in the car and by the look on his face that he had seen you girls in the grocery store. I'd seen that look so many times before. I told him I hoped he didn't plan to do anything stupid. They're neighbors, and they're just children. He spat at me and told me to shut up. I did. You see, you didn't cross Henry. You didn't look at Henry the wrong way, nor breathe the same air as Henry or you might receive a punch to the gut, or a kick in the ribs.

Looking back, I find it hard to believe that I had ever loved this man. He had been so handsome in his uniform the first

*day I saw him. I was attending a barn dance in Philo, and in
walked this tall, broad-shouldered guy with thick, sandy hair.
My heart skipped a beat. We were married six months later.
Exactly one week after that, I realized that I had made the
biggest mistake of my life. He and his father had become
nightmares of the worst kind. My parents told me I was now a
wife, and I should go home and make the best of it. I was so
desperate to get away from them, that I would pretend to hear
voices in my head and scream out, just to get them to take me to
the hospital. I was finally admitted to the state sanitorium in
Rantoul where the doctors diagnosed me with schizophrenia. I
was no more schizophrenic than the Man in the Moon, but if it
would keep me away from those monsters, I'd be anything I
needed to be. The only problem was that there were certain days
throughout the month that patients were granted family visits.
Those were the worst days because Henry hadn't had me
around for weeks, and he was storing up all that pent-up rage,
just for me.*

*That afternoon, when we saw you and Jenny at the store, he
had picked me up from Rantoul and, well, I could tell he was
in a quite a mood. I was hoping he'd just take it out on me like
he always did. But when we got home from the grocery store, he
ordered me into the house while he stayed outside. I asked him
to come on in. He answered me by punching me in the side and
shoving the grocery bag in my stomach.*

*I went in through the back door. "Ello, Enry!" That damned
bird had been taught to greet everyone with "Hello Henry" as
soon as someone entered or left. I hated that bird. Luther was
sitting in his chair, smoking his pipe, watching whatever was on
television. He barely looked up when I came in. I went to the
bathroom and checked my side for bruising. Sure enough, a
deep purple mark was already forming, just above my rib cage.
It was going to be a long few days. I stayed in the bathroom for*

as long as I could, twenty minutes or more. When I came out, Henry still hadn't come in. I peeked out the curtains hanging in the spare bedroom but didn't see him on the lawn anywhere. I went into the kitchen to make a cup of tea. I had just put the kettle on when I heard what sounded like a shrill scream of a wounded animal. I froze. I heard it again. I was about to go outside and look when the back door flew open, and there was Henry, holding Jenny. She was facing forward in his arms. One of his arms was holding her up around her waist, her feet dangling off the floor, and the other hand was covering her nose and mouth. Her eyes, oh my God! Her eyes showed sheer terror. She was flailing and kicking. I screamed at him to put her down and tried to pull her away from him. He used his body to slam me against the counter, leaving me in a puddle on the floor as he carried her into the other room. My head was throbbing and all I could hear was that damned bird, over and over, Ello Enry, Ello Enry, Ello Enry, with the muffled screams of Jenny in the background. I didn't know what to do. By the time I got to my feet, Henry had carried her into the bedroom and slammed the door. Luther managed to get up off his chair with the use of his cane. He was standing next to the side table, blocking my way. I told him to move. He laughed, he actually laughed at me and said something about that girl being quite a handful. I was horrified. I demanded again he move. He did not. I tried to get past him. He raised his cane above his head as if to strike me. It was then that I pushed him with all my might. I didn't look back to see what had happened. I just heard the thud. I ran into the spare bedroom and grabbed the gun that Henry kept in the top drawer. I knew it was loaded, and I knew how to use it. I went to the back bedroom and listened. I didn't hear anymore cries coming from behind the door. That scared me more than anything. I turned the knob and entered. There was Henry, straddling Jenny on the bed. His pants were down around his knees. He was raping her. I *told him to get up. He didn't stop. I told him again to get off her or I would put a bullet in his head. I backed up and cocked the gun. He got up, pulled his pants up, zipping them while never taking his eyes off me. Jenny began to stir. I was afraid he had killed her. He asked me what I was going to do now. He told me I didn't have the guts to pull the trigger. He told me I was nothing but a mouse. My hands began to shake. He started laughing. And the next thing I remember, the gun went off. He was dead. There was absolutely no doubt, half his head was gone. With both of us in shock, I helped your sister off the bed and led her to the bathroom. I could see Luther sprawled on the living room floor, but I blocked Jenny's view of him. I cleaned her up the best I could, wiping her forehead with a wet cloth and telling her she was going to be alright. Like me, she was shaking, not saying a word. I found my voice and told her she'd have to be strong now. That I was going to walk her out, but that she was to keep her eyes closed so that she no longer had to look at anymore ugliness. I asked her if she was okay to go home. She nodded yes. I told her that she was safe, that nobody would ever hurt her again. We walked around Luther to get to the back door. He wasn't moving. I could hear the train coming in the distance as I opened the door. I gave her a hug, and kissed the top of her head, but, before she left, that bird would utter its last words.*

I walked backed into the living room. I didn't know what to do. I had two dead bodies on my hands, a young girl had just been raped, and I was a psychiatric patient on furlough. Who would believe me, who would believe Jenny? So, I did what I could do. I staged the scene, making it look like Henry had killed himself. There wasn't much I could do about Luther, so I left him exactly where he had fallen. I waited until it got dark and went and knocked on Dorothy's back door. She was my friend, the only person who knew what was happening in my life. I was aware of how she felt about me. I cared for her, but not in the same way. She knew that. She took me in and said she would take care of everything anyway. She devised a plan to have me stay with her for a few days, hidden, until she could safely get me out of the city. I didn't even know she had asked your parents to help until right before I was to go. I was horrified that she had involved them. Dorothy said it was best that she and I not be seen together, so I was to go alone. She told your mother nothing except that I was an abused wife who would eventually be killed if I didn't get away. She hadn't been lying. She trusted your parents. Dorothy assured me that your parents knew nothing. She said that your sweet mother agreed to help without hesitation, and that it was apparent Jenny hadn't told a soul what had happened to her. We waited until late at night to avoid any possible contact with you kids. You would have already gone to bed. At least that was the plan, until you walked down the hall and found me standing in your living room.

I owe Dorothy and your parents my life. I don't know what would have happened to me if it weren't for their help. Dorothy eventually came to Brunswick and stayed by my side as a friend. I had told Anderson everything before we married. He loved me and protected me for the rest of my life. But Jenny, your sister—I failed her. I should have told someone. I should have told your parents. She should never have gone through that alone. I can only say I wish every day that I had handled things differently, but I can't go back. I'm sorry, Ellen. I really am. I do hope you can find it in your heart to forgive me for leaving your sister behind to deal with that trauma all by herself. I swear I would have done things differently if I could.

Respectfully,

Mae

I fell to my knees and screamed. I screamed and screamed until I had no more screams left. "Jenny, oh God, Jenny, I'm so sorry, I'm sorry," I sobbed. "I didn't know." I got back on my feet and staggered around in circles, the pages of the letter clutched to my chest. I stopped to catch my breath. I was hyperventilating. I managed to slow my breathing, only to begin hyperventilating all over again.

"Goddamn you, Mae, how could you, how could you have just left her like that? A child who had just been raped, and you send her on her way, all alone. What kind of a person does that? You're nothing but a complete phony, an imposter. I don't want your goddamned house! I don't want anything from you." I dropped to my knees and grabbed the peonies that Maggie had left on the grave and tore them to shreds. I pounded the headstone with my fists, and, finally, out of sheer exhaustion, I stopped. I just stopped. I sat with my back and head leaning against Madeline's headstone. Lilly, who had been watching me cross over into complete insanity, came and laid her head in my lap. I began to cry. I stroked her head and I cried. I didn't stop crying until I could no longer see out of either eye from the swelling. I finally pulled myself up off the ground and staggered to the bench. I knew this was going to take a long time to work through.

"How much could one little girl take?" I cried to Lilly.

Jenny and I had experienced so much that year. We were young, trying to make sense of a world that wasn't always kind and didn't care how old you were. But this, Jenny had to deal with this on top of everything else that had happened. I didn't know exactly how I would go forward. I would never tell Mom. There was no need for her to know. I'd think of some reason I'd asked her about Mae and Dorothy. I would tell Dan. I would need him as much as he would need me in the weeks and months ahead. As far as the house, well, I will leave that for another day. I couldn't think.

"C'mon, girl, it's time to go home." As I made my way down the hill, I heard the distinct caw of a bird. I stopped. Without looking back, I whispered, "Goodbye, Bird," and kept walking.

"I packed up the car and left the key in the service box. Lilly hopped in the back and settled on her blanket. I got in and found a station I liked. I rolled down the windows, punched in the code to open the gate, and headed out. I just had one stop to make before heading home.

"I promise, girl, I will only be a minute." I left the back windows down a crack and locked the doors. I signed in and made my way down the hall. Dorothy was in the exact spot I had left her days earlier. Only this time, she wasn't asleep. She was looking out the window, deep in thought.

"Hello, Dorothy."

She turned her head and studied my face. "Hello, Ellen," she finally said.

"I just want you to know that I know everything. I was given Mae's letter today. I'm going home."

"I suppose you hate us both," she said.

"Yes, I suppose I do. However, I know desperate people do desperate things. If it wasn't for Mae, my sister most likely would have died that day. As angry as I am, it must have taken a great deal of courage for Mae to fight off one man and shoot another."

"Oh, my dear," Dorothy said. "Mae didn't shoot Henry, Jenny did."

The End

ABOUT THE AUTHOR

Kim Wilson is a graduate of the University of Louisville with a Bachelors' Degree in Elementary Education and a Master's in Exceptional Child Education. This first-time author has been an educator for over twenty-five years. She is a wife, mother, and grandmother who adores her family and resides in Louisville, Kentucky. Find her at kimewilson.com.

51112965R00136

Made in the USA
Lexington, KY
31 August 2019